Don Pendleton

FIRST/SIGNER
25⁰⁰

**COPP
ON
FIRE**

COPP
ON
FIRE

By

DON PENDLETON

DONALD I. FINE, INC.
New York

This one's for Thomas,
who sees past the pretenses
that cloak the human heart,
and loves us for ourselves.
Remember me to the Doc.

D P

Library of Congress Cataloging-in-Publication Data

Pendleton, Don.
Copp on fire.

I. Title.
PS3566.E465C66 1988 813'.54 87-46278
ISBN 1-55611-088-X

Manufactured in the United States of America
10 9 8 7 6 5 4 3 2 1

"I never met a man I didn't like."
—*Will Rogers, American Humorist*

". . . I, the unloving,
say life should be lovely."
—*Vachel Lindsay, American Poet*

"I never met a man I didn't like,
until he takes a whack at me. Then
I love the bastard, after I whack
him back, for reminding me that life
ought to be lovelier than it usually is."
—*Joe Copp, American Private Eye*

CHAPTER ONE

Death is unlovely, sure, but life is sometimes even more so. And I have known crimes against the spirit far more terrible in their total effect than any trespass upon mere flesh. Crime is my business, you see—and every time I reach the point where I think I've seen it all, something new comes along to confound and stupefy the professional senses.

But I'm ahead of myself already. My name really is Joe Copp. I'm licensed by the state of California as a private investigator. I was a public cop for eighteen years and I did it all—robbery, narcotics, vice, homicide, name it. It's an unlovely life, but I guess it's all I ever really wanted to do with mine, so by that standard I'm a successful and contented man. Most of the time. I have my ups and downs, like anyone else. By and large, I'm okay. I do like it better since I've been calling my own shots. I lost all the financial security when I went private, of course, but some things are just more important than financial security—like freedom, for example. I take my freedom seriously, and I came to the realization long ago that you just cannot get freedom and security together in most packages.

So I'm a private cop now. I answer only to myself and to my own conscience. I've got one of those, sure, and I try to let it be my guide. Sometimes I screw it up, but never on purpose. Well . . . hardly ever.

I don't take every job that comes along. Don't work for divorce lawyers or ambulance chasers, and I don't do routine insurance investigations or skiptracing. Right away there I've eliminated the beans and potatoes work that keeps most private cops in business, but I'm not in this for beans and potatoes. I prefer criminal cases. That kind of work usually comes to me through criminal lawyers, public defenders and the like operating on limited budgets, so it's not particularly lucrative. So I guess I'm not really working for the money, am I? I work for the work, and for the luxury of picking my own.

There are other moments, of course, when I snarl at myself and lecture myself to be more financially responsible. These tend to be weak moments, financially threatening moments—like, you mean the rent is due again already?

It was, and the bank account was nearly flat, and I was snarling at myself for being so damned self-righteous when that stretch limousine hove into view. You need to get a mental picture of this. I share this small business complex in the San Gabriel Valley with a barber, a beautician, a realtor, an accountant, a dress shop and several other small-time businesses—all at ground level. We have a 7-11 store at one entrance and a gas station at the other. It's that kind of place. You know what I mean. Neither uptown or downtown—it's notown—twenty-five minutes east of the L. A. civic center, and the only real winner there is the landlord because most of the tenants are hanging onto the leases by their fingernails just like me.

So into this scene of quiet desperation let us roll a stretch limousine, a gleamingly white Lincoln about twenty-four feet long with tinted windows and a uniformed chauffeur. It is midafternoon and the 7-11 area is alive with kids who congregate and dawdle there on weekdays enroute between school and home. I have nothing against kids as long as they are a respectful minority among adults but I get a bit nervous in social situations where they outnumber us on our own turf, so on afternoons like that one I spend a lot of time at my office window where I can keep an eye on the little darlings as they spill into my parking area with their slurpees and quart-size cokes and what have you.

Which is why I spotted the limousine coming in. My first idle thought was that the guy picked a hell of a place to run out of cigarettes because he'd have to stand in line behind twenty grabassing kids balancing (or not) a doomsday confection in each hand. You'll know what I mean by that term if you've ever had a slurpee poured down the inside of your pants.

Anyway, I figured the limousine for a quickstop at 7-11 but instead it nosed on through the juvenile jungle and halted right outside my door, astride four parking spaces. I couldn't see through the tinted glass so of course I had no idea who might be inside that yacht but I did not particularly give a damn either. All I knew was that the jerk was standing across all my parking spaces and it irritated me. Not that I was *saving* the space for anyone in particular; no one had parked there all week—but what the hell, there could be a rush, couldn't there?—and then where would all my clients park?

So I was about ready to step outside and yell about the encroachment when the chauffeur beat me to the punch. Dark, goodlooking guy of about twenty-five maybe, immaculate in his uniform and energetic in his body language, he left the engine idling and made a beeline to my door. I have this small reception area but no receptionist, also no secretary or help of any kind. I do it all myself with no trouble whatever because it takes only one to do nothing— and that is most of what I was doing at the time.

So I opened the door to my inner office at about the same time the chauffeur was coming through the outer doorway. I am figuring this guy has the wrong address; this is a limousine for hire and he's trying to find his pickup. I am in a lousy mood because I am bored and also a bit depressed over the cash-flow situation—all of the flow was in the wrong direction and the pool was slowly drying up—so I am ready to come down hard on the guy for tying up my parking spaces.

But he showed me a respectful smile as he inquired, "Are you Mr. Copp?"

I admitted it.

He said, "Mr. Moore would like to talk to you. In the car."

I was thinking *thank you, God* but I guess my lousy mood was in charge of my mouth because my brilliant response was: "Tell your Mr. Moore to call for an appointment. I'll see when I can work him in."

What the hell, I was thinking, I'm not a drive-up dick. Whattaya mean, *in the car?* I don't give curb service. I don't . . .

The chauffeur was reading me, I guess. His gaze flicked about the modest office and the smile hung in there as he replied, "Mr. Moore is physically handicapped. He would appreciate it very much if you would extend him the courtesy . . ."

So I end up in the limousine with this so-called Albert Moore. He is a concoction from a casting director's vision of a Beverly Hills mogul. A car robe covers his lap and legs. He is about fifty, give or take a couple—roundfaced, balding, a bit overweight, dressed like bankers used to dress except that the eyes are concealed behind heavily smoked glasses. I hate talking business with anyone who is hiding behind those damned things—but then, a lot of people are hiding out these days.

The mogul is not the only one present. A beautifully blond-and-tanned young woman is seated beside him. I think of an ostrich when I look at her because she is wearing the dark glasses, too, but the eyes are about the only thing she is hiding. She's dressed, sure, but in a way calculated to reveal instead of cover up, and there is much to be revealed here. Very long and shapely legs, as item one, visible all the way to the crotch beneath a mini that was not designed for sitting, for item two, and one of those criss-cross swatches of silky material that merely drape a free-standing bosom as the clincher.

I folded my six-three/two-sixty onto a little jump seat, facing them, and looked them over as they looked me over.

The guy introduced himself but not the woman. The voice was dry, reedy, almost pained—but the brain behind it seemed hard as nails, and it got right down to business.

"I want you for a ten-hour job, Mr. Copp."

"Starting when?"

"Eight o'clock tomorrow morning. Can you handle cameras?"

I looked him over for another moment before replying, "Any kind I can hold in my hand, yeah. What are we photographing?"

"A disloyal employee, I suspect," he said with a little sigh. "Perhaps more than one. I want you to conceal yourself outside a business location in Hollywood and photograph every person entering and leaving the premises. You supply the camera and the film. Use a telephoto lens and get good tight closeups of the faces. I want to see their freckles, you understand. And they are not to know that they are being photographed. Can you handle that?"

I was not so sure that I wanted to handle it. Well okay, sure, I needed the work. But . . .

I told the guy, "A ten-hour stakeout is not my idea of a fun day, Mr. Moore—and of course I would have to shove all my other work aside, and it's across town, so—"

"Name your price."

"I don't work cheap. It will cost you a thou."

"Very well."

He had bought the fee too quickly, so I bumped it a bit. I really didn't want the job, you see. "That covers my time. Expenses are extra. And the travel— that's another hundred, each way. The film and the processing—"

"Add another hundred for the film and the use of your equipment, but there will be no processing. You are to deliver the undeveloped film at precisely ten minutes past the hour of six tomorrow evening." He produced a manila envelope. "These are your full instructions." He counted out thirteen crisp hundreds from a breast-pocket wallet and put them in the envelope. "Cash in advance. Follow the written instructions to the letter. There will be no need for us to meet again. I trust you to do the job properly."

I accepted the envelope with misgivings. This was not my kind of work, and I did not like the smell of it. But the rent was due again, and I was beginning to like this guy. I found the lady interesting too. There was a winsomeness to these two, and sort of a vulnerability that invites gentle handling. Still, it didn't feel just right for me.

"You say your name is Albert Moore?"

He showed me a faint smile. "That is what I said, yes."

"What are you going to do with the pictures?"

"That's my business."

"Mine too. I do have a license to consider. And even a conscience."

The smile was fading as he replied, "A private detective with a conscience? Come on now, Mr. Copp. It is no crime to take pictures."

"It can be," I argued, "if the pictures are to be used for illegal purposes."

He frowned and took back the envelope. "You haven't earned a thousand dollars all this month," he told me in that pained, almost wounded, voice.

That was an item of truth, and I doubted that the guy was shooting in the dark. Probably he'd checked me out, and not necessarily for my credentials only. We sat in a sort of strained silence for what seemed like a minute but probably was only a few seconds, the two of them staring at me from behind their shades and obviously waiting to see which way the thing was going to turn. I picked up an anxiety there. The sensing I got was that I was in control, so I told the guy, "I have good months and bad ones. So I'm having a bad one. All that proves is that I'm hungry, not that I'll eat anything that comes along. So if you drove all the way over here thinking—"

He stopped me with a hand on my knee. That will always stop me, coming from male or female, but for different reasons.

"Your ethics are what attracted me to you, Mr. Copp. This is a delicate matter for me—highly delicate—but please believe that I am not asking you to become involved in anything illegal or even unethical. I've come to you because I have been assured that you are both reliable and discreet, but of course also because—"

"Who told you that?"

"But also because you don't stand on formality. Just take the damned pictures for me, will you? You don't need my life history for that, do you?"

"I don't want your history," I replied. "But I do want to know how you intend to use the pictures."

He turned to the woman then quickly back to me with another pained smile as he told me, "My business is highly competitive. Someone within my own organization is ripping me off. I want to know who is doing it. I have set a trap. The guilty party or parties shall find reason to visit this Hollywood address during business hours tomorrow. If I can just learn who they are, then I can use them to turn the tables in a fitting manner. It's as simple, and proper, as that."

"You'll just keep quiet about it and feed disinformation to the traitor."

"Something like that, yes."

"Why didn't you just say that in the first place?" He again offered the envelope and I accepted it. We even shook hands, and I told my new client: "You'll have your pictures."

Not that I had bought the whole gag but because I wanted to believe the "simple and proper" bit. Maybe he was looking for an industrial spy, maybe not. Maybe he was looking for a cheating wife or mistress, maybe anything. You never really know, sometimes. What you try to do is cover your ass . . . and, pardon the expression, your conscience.

I needed the job so I bought the gag. That was not the only reason but it figured strongly, and even my conscience knew later that I should not have bought it. There was nothing fitting or proper about it. My client had murder in the heart. This job set my soul on fire. It is not a very pretty story, but . . .

Get comfortable and let me tell you about it.

CHAPTER TWO

So the gag was an all-day surveillance of this shabby little storefront in a rundown section of Hollywood. The weathered sign out front identified the business as *NuCal Designs* and placards that nearly covered the windows gave evidence that they dealt with theatrical costuming and the like.

The location presented no problem. My van has one-way glass on both sides. I arrived early enough to get a good position at the curb with an unobstructed angle on the entrance to the building, and I had plenty of time to set up my equipment and prepare for the surveillance. My Mr. Moore was a bit behind the times. We don't do photo-surveillance with still cameras so much anymore. Mostly we use video equipment, and the technology has become so fine that we can get decent tape at one-half-lux lighting, which is about like the light from a birthday candle. I didn't bother to tell the client about that. He wanted stills, so stills he would get, and I had good equipment for that too—but I also set up the video equipment for my own backup.

Moore had not asked for sound, either, but I went ahead and aligned the audio barrels, which can pick a conversation off a windowpane from a distance.

All this is standard surveillance routine. I wasn't trying to be cute. This is the way it's done, easy as pie. After the setups I sit up front in comfort with the remotes and anyone passing by or even looking in wouldn't know what is going on there.

The van itself is never a problem, either. Magnetic decals go on and off in·a whisk, and I have several different sets. For this job, in a business environment, I used *Southland Communications,* suggesting a private telephone outfit—of which, now, there are many in this area. The meter maids tend to look the other way if it's a public-utility-type vehicle at the curb, and actually the utility vans are becoming as common as taxicabs in today's complex urban environments and so they seldom raise an eyebrow in any setting.

I had only two subjects during the first hour—both store employees—none at all the second hour and only four across the balance of the morning.

Quite a yawn. The client wanted a log—he'd even provided the forms for it—showing the precise time at which each frame of film was exposed. My camera does that automatically, actually imprinting the time of exposure on the film itself, so I scrawled "See Film" across the printed form and put it back in the envelope. Once the telephoto lens was focused on the setup mark, all I had to do was sit there in my captain's seat and press the remote shutter button at the appropriate times. The video took care of itself; all I had to do was change the tape a few times and I lost nothing during those brief episodes.

It was not my idea of a fun day. There was a bit of a flurry during the lunch hour, but by two o'clock—halfway through the surveillance period—I had pushed the button on a total of four men and ten women, none of them especially remarkable or memorable. I did not push it again until a few seconds past six as the employees were locking up and departing.

It had been a totally uneventful and crashingly boring day, all that I had expected it to be.

I delivered the exposed film per the printed instructions, passing it off to the same uniformed chauffeur of the same limousine at the corner of Melrose and La Brea at precisely ten minutes past the hour. He was alone in the car and acknowledged the delivery with nothing but a grin as he eased on around the corner with the film in his lap.

I went on up the street and found a pancake house for some quick food—I'd had nothing but a dry sandwich all day—and I was sitting there within five minutes of the job when the whole area came alive with sirens and the heavy rumble of firefighting equipment. It was now nearly seven o'clock and I was dawdling over coffee, content to kill some time and allow the early evening traffic to relax a bit before heading home.

But all the noise and a glow in the sky coaxed me back onto the streets and flowing with it back toward the scene of the day's activities. I could not get within two blocks of it. I did learn that there had been a massive explosion and that a whole row of buildings were burning. By the time I worked my way to the barricades on foot, it appeared that half the city's firefighters and ambulances were on the scene and still the sirens were howling in.

I satisfied myself that *NuCal Designs* was indeed at the heart of that conflagration and I even had a few words with a fire captain and a guy from arson, enough to produce a bit of nausea in the pit of my stomach. These guys were talking *bomb,* numerous casualties.

I returned to the valley and went to work on my videotapes. I had ten hours of mostly nothing on those tapes, compressible to about fifteen minutes of meaningful activity, but there also could be useful peripheral activity—both video and audio—and I wanted to see if the impersonal staring eye of that camera had recorded anything that my own glazed-over eyes had missed.

I have a pretty neat video-processing lab, thanks to a client who couldn't afford my tab but wanted to show his appreciation and was no longer into the video game anyway, so passed his toys on in lieu of cash. I don't normally barter for services, but I have to say that I came out on the better end of that deal. I can edit, mix, combine, amplify and copy at high speed, add text and all sorts of special effects—just about anything the pros can do—and I do make good use of this equipment. I keep it at home because there's more room there, but it is part of my business inventory.

Still, it was close onto midnight before I'd satisfied myself that there was nothing obviously hot on those tapes. Two different subjects had carried small pack-ages into *NuCal Designs* but both were women and both had carried similar packages out with them. There was nothing else of any real interest on the tapes. I copied the pieces I wanted and took the original tapes over to the sheriff's station and left them along with an explanatory note for a friend in the detective division, Ken Forta. Used to work with the guy, and we keep in touch.

In case you're wondering about confidentiality and the client relationship, forget it. All that goes out the window in a situation like this. Besides, I was already beginning to feel that I had been used somehow and maybe compromised, somehow, by this "client" who undoubtedly had come to me under a false name in a hired limousine. I had taken the precaution of noting the license tag on that boat—it's an easy one: *Star 5,* and I left that for Forta too.

I didn't really know what to think about any of it. I just felt vaguely uneasy and was taking some precautions to help keep myself clean in the matter, whatever the matter was.

There was nothing but a formless worry in my own gut to connect my surveillance of the day with the explosion and fire that followed. It could be coincidence, even if it did turn out that the building had indeed been bombed. Moore's "trap" could be as innocent as he claimed, and maybe the guy would check out clean.

I was pulled out of bed by a call from Forta at seven the next morning. He told me that *Star 5* was the property of *Starway Limousines* of Hollywood—and when had I last seen that car?

I told him.

He said, "That's very interesting."

"What's so interesting?"

"The vehicle was destroyed by a car-bomb at about eight o'clock last night," he informed me as only a cop can do when he's speaking for effect. "So were its two occupants."

"Really."

"Uh huh. The boss wants words with you, Joe. Come on in."

So of course I went on in. I was involved, it seemed, in something considerably less benign than a disinformation campaign. Could I even be regarded as an accessory to murder?

If so I could stop worrying about the financial-security angle. The state takes full care of all us stupid folk.

I didn't know what I'd done, for whom or to what effect. And I was scared to find out.

CHAPTER THREE

I had a rough two hours with the county of Los Angeles. Forta's boss is not what most of us would call a nice guy. He's vain, self-important, politically ambitious. We had equal rank when I was with the county, but even then he was commanding a desk downtown and we had occasion to butt heads a few times. Now he's a division commander—but I'm not going to say which one and I'm not even going to call the guy by his real name; he's the kind that would sue me. Let's just call him Edgar.

I met Forta at the substation and we went downtown in his car. Edgar had a hard-on for LAPD. He'll never pass up an opportunity to embarrass them in any small way, and he near trembles like with passion over a chance to upstage them. I think this all started when Daryl Gates, the L. A. chief, snubbed Edgar at a joint press conference some years back. That is how small this guy is.

Anyway, I tumbled real quick to his movement with me. My office is located in an area that is under the direct jurisdiction of the sheriff's department; my town contracts the services from the county. The two bombing incidents—which right now were the hottest items in town—occurred in LAPD jurisdiction. My possible involvement in the bombings opened the door for Edgar to launch an independent investigation.

This guy was in hot pursuit for my butt and I knew it. He wanted to at least establish a reasonable basis for an interest in the case, one that he could sell upstairs.

So, as I said, I had a rough two hours.

Edgar *knew* that I had not consciously conspired to kill, maim or inflame in Hollywood. But he did want to entertain the notion, and he's clever enough to put together a few little inconsistencies to make it look like maybe I had.

Why, for example, should someone pay me thirteen hundred dollars to take fourteen snapshots of a building he was going to burn down that same evening?

Obviously, I replied, the two events are not connected.

Then why did I elect to betray confidentiality and turn my evidence over if I had not thought there was a connection?

Because I had thought that possibly the camera could have picked up something that would lead to the identity of the bomber, so I wanted to make it available for close scrutiny.

Why had I not turned the tape over to my client?

Because the client had not contracted for the tape. He'd asked for stills. He got the stills.

Well, if the client had not contracted the tape, why had I gone to all that trouble to create the tape?

It was no trouble at all. The equipment was right there. I used it.

To what end?

For my own records. (Weak, weak.)

Do I always keep such records?

Not always.

So why this time?

Well, I really knew nothing about the client, and he was acting mysterious and didn't even want me to see my own pictures . . . No, that's not right, a lot of afterthought is coloring this—I had nothing like that in mind at the time—it was just a backup, that's all, a backup in case the other equipment went haywire.

But I'd just said that I don't always use backup systems.

I'd just said no such damned thing. What I said is that I don't always keep a videotape record. Back off. I think it should be very obvious why I brought in this tape. Now if you can't see the obvious then give me back my damned tape. I didn't come in here to . . .

Sure, I played right into his arrogant little hands. He pushed my buttons and I reacted the way he knew I would. Now he's got a belligerent suspect in hand and he's beginning to squeeze.

If I'd completed the assignment at six o'clock and delivered the film a few minutes later, how is it that I was still on the scene when the building blew at seven o'clock?

Had I actually placed the film in the chauffeur's

hand at the corner of Melrose and La Brea?—or didn't I in fact get into the limo at that point for another meeting with my client? And was there really any film, after all?

Could I verify my whereabouts during the two hours between six o'clock, when I completed the assignment, and eight o'clock, when the limousine exploded and killed its two occupants?

Did I in fact shoot that video on the day in question, or was it shot at some prior time to check out the movements in and around that doomed building?

Could I offer any explanation for why my client was killed in a second bombing even before the flames from the first had subsided?—and would I consider that a deliberate act of murder or as an ironic accident?

And would I, finally, keep myself available for further questions in the matter?

I told the guy to go to hell and went out of there in a rage. Forta was sympathetic, but after we'd returned to his car he pointed out, "He did ask some valid questions there, Joe."

I had to admit that was true.

I also knew that I was lucky to walk out of there with my license intact. It takes a full hearing to revoke it entirely—and some very good evidence of criminality or "malfeasance" to make it stick—but any department anywhere in the state can temporarily suspend a license in their jurisdiction, pending formal charges.

I told Ken Forta, "Valid questions, sure, but the guy already knows the answers. He just wants to stand on my nose to reach into Daryl's cookie jar, and you know it as well as I do. I asked you to convey that tape to LAPD, Ken. Why didn't you do it?"

"I did, after I made a copy for the boss. I've been up all night on this thing. It's going to be a hot potato, make no mistake about it, especially once the facts are made public."

"What facts are those?"

"Well, I mean, you know, the true identity of your client."

I was getting the tickles at the back of the neck. "What true identity is that?"

"Well, I just meant—I figured you knew—one of the men who died in the limousine—you didn't know that?"

"Know *what?*"

"It was Bernie Wiseman."

"*What* Bernie Wiseman?! The guy at—?"

"The president at United Talents, yeah. *That* Bernie Wiseman. You didn't know? Joe, I figured you were just standing on confidentiality. You really didn't know?"

Of course not. I really did not know a thing. I was just a hungry jerk hired by the wonder boy of motion pictures to close a trap on his enemies, and the trap had closed on him—maybe me, too—before I could even know who I was looking for.

United Talents under Wiseman had scored box-office smash after smash and was moving in on the network and pay-television markets.

Wiseman had just survived an inside power play to oust him as head of the studio. He'd been reconfirmed by his board of directors and given an even stronger hand in his stated determination to dominate the entertainment industry, and he'd been the talk of the town for weeks.

All that, of course, was strictly outside my league so I knew nothing but the name and the talk.

So how was I supposed to recognize the guy when he came calling in a rented limo and a false identity?

It would take a while to quiet my head and try to pull the pieces together.

As it turned out, I did not have that kind of time. I'd been written into a crazy Hollywood script as an entirely expendable character. I would have to awaken to that truth very soon . . . or burn with it.

CHAPTER FOUR

Forta took me on over to the city of Los Angeles
and introduced me to Abe Johnson, the guy in
charge of the investigation for LAPD. Johnson
gave me an enthusiastic handshake and acted like
we were old friends too long parted. I couldn't remember him. He asked, "How does it feel to run
naked through the wild and woolly jungle with no
paydays and no benefit package?"

"Wild and woolly . . ." I said, trying to place the guy.
I was with the city for a while, some years back, and
I was sure I'd never worked with the guy; my memory
is not that bad. Johnson is black and a native of Ar-
kansas, big guy with an engaging smile and interested eyes. LAPD does not hire upper ranks from
outside the department, they promote from within. I
approve of that. You don't make lieutenant quickly at
LAPD, so I knew that the guy had been around for a
while. Maybe we'd met once at a departmental social,

a picnic or ballgame. Whatever, I liked this cop right off.

He said, "Thanks for the tape, Joe. The lab boys have been scrutinizing it all day."

"Anything yet?"

"Some interesting murmurs now and then on the soundtrack."

"Well, you're ahead of me there. I didn't take time to screen the audio, just ran a quick scan and picked off the video subjects for my own file before surrendering the tape. What kind of murmurs?"

"Oh, very angry sounds—from the interior of the shop, we presume. What kind of mike were you using?"

"Directional barrels. So the audio pickup was directly off the shop windows."

"They'd rattle from either direction though, wouldn't they."

"Yeah, but differently. Your technicians will be able to tell the difference. It's subtle but—"

"Well, we thank you for the tape. It could mean a lot. We got another break, too, a lead on a young woman who apparently was involved."

I had a quick mental picture of long legs and impenetrable sunglasses. I pulled out a chair and sat down and told all to Abe Johnson.

He jotted notes as I talked, nodding his head in agreement with certain information that seemed to coincide with something else he already had, but no questions and no interruptions until I'd told what I had. Then he told me what he had. I was liking the guy more and more.

"That ties pretty well. Your blond is probably the same woman we're looking for. Her name is Melissa

Franklin. She's an actress and she's been seen a lot recently with Wiseman."

"How did you tie her in?"

"She was observed by one of our traffic units getting out of the limousine just moments before it exploded. She moved to another vehicle that was parked at the curb just behind the limousine. The kids on traffic detail would never miss one like this. Our boy watched her pull away and even noted the license plate on her car. He was half a block down the street and right behind her when the limousine blew. She kept right on going but he doubled back immediately to cover the trouble."

"But he had her tags."

"He had 'em—we love these personalized tags, you know. They stay in the mind."

"I'd like to meet the lady."

"Don't worry, you will. Soon as we run her down. Hasn't lived at her DMV address for more than six months. Wiseman's place is in Bel Air, and apparently he lived alone. The housekeeper knows Melissa Franklin but not much about her. But we'll run her down."

I glanced at Ken Forta as I asked Johnson, "Is there any question about the car bomb? Could it have been accidental?"

"We wondered about that after we got your report—but the explosives were fixed to the frame of the vehicle and wired to a timer. It blew straight up through the floorboards, the gas tank exploded too. Made a mess, Joe. We were lucky to get ID on the victims."

"How good is that ID?"

"Good enough. Wiseman had hired the car for the

day but he took it as your same Albert Moore. That corroborates your report. He wanted to pay cash but he also wanted to use his own driver, so the agency insisted on a cash or credit security deposit equal to the replacement value of the vehicle. So the guy calling himself Albert Moore shows up with a credit bond drawn on United Talents under the signature of Bernard Wiseman. In other words, the studio is guaranteeing the security of the vehicle but it's checked out to Albert Moore."

"And the driver?"

"The driver is Albert Moore. We've verified his chauffeur's permit with DMV."

"No—you see, Abe—Albert Moore is—"

"I know, I know." Johnson waved me off. "But there really *is* an Albert Moore—or *was*—and he really was a chauffeur on United Talents' payroll, drove a limo every day almost identical to the Starway vehicle. Moore rented the limo and United Talents guaranteed the security. Maybe it sounds too cutesy but it would work to keep Wiseman's name out of the record if things had gone okay. So what do you think was going on, Joe? Why did Wiseman go to all that trouble to conceal his identity?"

"Seems obvious. I get it a lot. Bashful clients, I mean. As for the rented limo, same logic. He didn't want to use a car that could be traced to his true identity . . . I'd like to see the remains."

"Be my guest, but even his own mother wouldn't recognize . . ."

"So how'd you ID?"

"Mostly medical and dental records, but there were other bits to nail it down."

"Any chance it was *not* Bernie Wiseman in that car?"

"I'm satisfied it's him," Johnson said. "He left the studio with Moore at noon yesterday and hasn't been seen since." He opened a folder, produced an eight-by-ten color photo, handed it to me. "That your man?"

I couldn't be sure. The man pictured in that studio still seemed a bit younger and thinner than the one I'd faced in that limo outside my office. The hair and style looked the same. I tried to visualize the face in the photo with dark glasses covering the eyes, still couldn't be sure.

"Was Wiseman physically handicapped?"

"Paralyzed from the waist down."

"It's him."

"Sure?"

"No."

"Pretty sure?"

"Almost."

"What are you making, Joe?"

"Find out what the head of United Talents would gain by staging his own death."

"Okay. On the surface I'd say nothing. He's been riding the top of the wave around here lately. Worth much more alive than dead."

"You sure?"

"No, but it figures."

I stood up, looked at Forta, told Johnson: "I'd figure it some more. You asked about the wild and woolly? I can pick my own, pal, that's how it is. I would not pick this one."

We chatted a bit more as Johnson escorted Forta

and me outside. I learned that the arson team was still at work in the bombed-out building and that they were saying nothing pending their final conclusions; Johnson was a bit irritated about that because he had two homicides connected with that one too—derelicts who'd been buried under the debris in the alleyway. The three of us hoo-hooed a bit about the agonies of conflicting personalities and the division of responsibilities in criminal investigations, then Forta took me back to my car and I asked him about Abe Johnson along the way.

"You don't remember him?"

I said I couldn't place him.

"That's weird," Forta said.

"Why?"

"He's the guy."

"What guy?"

"The guy that Angie was . . . involved with when she divorced you. I think they're married now."

"Well, I never met the man. That's why I didn't recognize him."

"That all you have to say about it?"

"What'd you expect?"

"Well, you spoiled all my fun. I kept waiting for you to wake up and put the guy on his ass."

"Hey, we're talking seven, eight years ago. Besides, he seemed like a nice guy."

"I don't believe it. You're not the same guy I used to know, Joe."

"I hope not."

"That guy was screwing your wife."

"She was screwing him back. The marriage was dead before that started."

"You've really changed, pal," Forta said with a disappointed sigh.

Not really, not all that much. Don't know how I got the reputation as a hardass. Angela tried to be a proper wife and I tried to be a proper husband, but it fell apart. I think maybe I could make marriage work now. But I don't expect to try again. No reason why Angela shouldn't. And I really did like Abe Johnson.

The question I would have to ask myself was did Abe Johnson like me? Because I was going to be needing all the support I could get, from wherever.

The missing Melissa Franklin was waiting outside my office when I got back, scared and looking for protective arms.

So much for the wild and woolly jungle and picking your own fights.

It is not a one-way world. What goes around, comes around. And sometimes the fight picks you.

CHAPTER FIVE

Melissa Franklin was one hell of a beautiful woman, and there was something even beyond beauty that reached out and touched you by her close presence, a magnetic sort of something that made you want to get even closer. A tall girl, mid to late twenties, with the new-woman fitness look, an aerobics workout look, and you knew that even her sweat would smell good.

The car she was driving fit the image very well, and it was as memorable as its tags. Personalized plates on the red Jaguar XJ-6 proclaimed that someone had PAID DUES for the pleasure of driving it, but none of that joy was presently in evidence. Our eyes met as I pulled in beside the Jag and I could see misery and fear flare into something like relief or hopeful anticipation before she clouded the gaze and covered the emotion with a blank stare.

She reacted immediately and unlocked her door on

the passenger side when I rapped the window with a knuckle, but she averted the gaze when I slid onto the seat beside her. I kept one foot on the ground and the door open—as much to reassure the lady as anything else—and I gave her a chance to speak first, but she didn't seem to know how to start, so I started for her.

"Waiting for me, Melissa?"

She kept her attention on the steering wheel. "Yes, but I'm not sure I know why. How did you know my name?"

"A traffic cop made you leaving the scene just before the limo exploded. They want to talk to you. You need to go in."

She sat with shoulders hunched, hands on the steering wheel while I wondered what was going on inside her lovely head. She was dressed in a leather jumpsuit with slits up the legs. Her top had a neckline that plunged. When she turned her eyes onto me they sent electricity.

"Promise me you'll never wear sunglasses again."

"What?"

"I couldn't see your eyes the other day. They're too good to hide."

"I don't understand."

"When you came here with Bernie."

"I've never seen you before in my life," she said in a tone usually reserved for a statement of the obvious.

I chewed that for a moment. "So why are you seeing me now?"

"I'm trying to find Bernie."

"If you've never seen me before in your life, how'd you know to start looking here—and how do you even know who I am?"

She tossed that golden head and gave me a side-wise flash from the eyes. "I've known about you from the beginning," she told me. "I helped Bernie select you. Now I want you to help me find him. I'll retain you. Name your price. I can afford it."

I ran a hand along the leathered interior of the Jag and replied, "I'm sure you can. But there's no need. I don't know your game, Melissa, but I know that you know that Bernie is dead. You were within sight of it when his car blew up last night. So why would you be trying to find him here? The county morgue is—"

"*Stop* that. The man in that car was not Bernie Wiseman. You know that as well as I do."

"I know nothing," I replied quietly, patiently. If it wasn't Bernie, then who?"

She was teary. "Don't try to tell me that you weren't in on this, I know all about it—"

"Exactly what do you think you know?"

"I know that Bernie was coming to see you. He was setting something up, I know that. And I was sup-posed to meet him in Hollywood last night, after-ward. I know that. But the man in the car wasn't Bernie. So where is he?"

I took my time lighting a cigarette, then blew the smoke outside. "This is getting ridiculous, kid."

She agreed, but with a lot less patience than I was showing. "It sure is!"

"Let's start it again. You and Wiseman came here two days ago in a rented limo and under false colors. He posed as a man named Albert Moore and hired me to sit outside *NuCal Designs* and photograph the comings and goings all day yesterday. I delivered the film to his chauffeur at a few minutes past six. At about seven o'clock *NuCal* blew and took most of the neighborhood with it. An hour later the rented limo blew and took Wiseman and his chauffeur with it. But it didn't take you with it, because you beat it away from there moments before the blow. A traffic cop saw you transfer to this car and he made a note of your license tags. The homicide people are interested in your close escape, they want to talk to you about that. It would look better if you found them instead of vice versa."

It was late afternoon. I wanted to get inside and check my machine for calls while there was still some business time left in the day. It wasn't that I was indifferent to this lady's problem; I just did not see that I could add anything worthwhile to her game on her terms. So I left her sitting there in her emotional stew and I went on into my office.

She followed quickly and joined me inside before I could get through the reception area.

"They want to kill me too!" she announced breathlessly. You've got to help me!"

I gave her a cold stare as I replied, "I don't have to do a damned thing, kid. But I've been known to do quite a lot when I'm properly asked."

"I'm asking you," she said miserably.

"Didn't hear it," I said. "What did you ask?"

"Will you help me?" she muttered.

I opened the inner office and invited her inside. I didn't know if I could help her or not. The lady certainly had my attention, though and I was willing to try. But then something rushed out of the office behind me and exploded against my head with a flash of pain and nausea. I grasped the significance of that feeling but I could not follow it intellectually; it felt like death, like dying and spinning into a bottomless chasm and being too sick to care. I must have gone out like a light because I do not even remember hitting the floor.

I came out of it with Ken Forta and two uniformed deputies bending over me. I felt very sick and very weak, and my head was like ten Margarita hangovers. Someone growled, "Look out, he's going to puke," and someone helped me turn onto my side. I retched a couple of times but nothing came up. The nausea began fading, though, and I became aware of blood in my hair.

I sat up and put a hand to the wound, couldn't feel any brain tissue spilling out, decided I'd live. Someone grabbed my hand and slapped a cuff on it.

Forta growled, "Take that off!—take it off!"—and the cuff magically slipped away.

I muttered, "What the hell is going down, Ken?" and tried to get to my feet but couldn't even find my feet.

Forta said, "Sit still, Joe. For God's sake, just sit there and behave yourself until the medics get here."

I said, "No, no, you don't understand," but then neither did I. It was all jumbled and weird, and it became even more so. I think probably I was slipping in and out of consciousness, because I don't remember seeing the paramedics until we were inside the ambulance, then I saw them again at the trauma center as I was being wheeled into the surgery.

It all came back, in there, as the doctor and two nurses were doing things to my head. I saw Ken Forta standing just outside the door with a worried face and the two deputies leaning lazily against a wall and looking bored. I called over, "Ken! Is the girl okay?"

He just smiled at me, and a nurse shushed me, and the doc went on doing things to my scalp.

I yelled, "Goddammit, Ken! Is she okay?"

The nurse again tried to intervene but the doctor told her, "It's okay, we're finished. Let the officer come in." He told Forta, "Superficial, he'll mend. He's all yours."

I wondered what he meant by that, but I should have known by the look on Forta's face.

The uniforms came into the room while Forta recited my rights to me.

I said, "What the hell is this?"

He said, "Sorry, Joe. It's a collar. Suspicion of homicide."

"Aw no," I said. "She was alive and well when my lights went out. I had nothing to do with it."

He told me, "I believe you, Joe, even though I don't know what you're talking about." He bent down to whisper, "Shut up, dammit, until you've got your lawyer."

Then the uniforms pulled me off the table and cuffed me.

It became very real, then. It was not a nightmare. It was entirely real, and I was under arrest for murder.

The charge was conspiracy to murder. The list of victims was long, and growing hourly.

But Bernard Wiseman and Melissa Franklin were not on that list.

CHAPTER SIX

Edgar's charges were several pages long. He was challenging the medical identification of Wiseman and he was trying to tie me to a criminal conspiracy.

According to Edgar's theory of the case, Wiseman had enlisted my services in an effort to identify certain business enemies and then to eliminate them.

Quite a few had been eliminated.

I was surprised to learn that five had died in the *NuCal* bombing—the two indigents that I mentioned earlier plus another three John Does of whom bits and pieces were discovered inside the building.

Another two John Does died in the limo.

Four more connected persons had died during the next twenty-four hours—three women and a man, all of whose names meant nothing whatever to me. I'd just taken their pictures during my surveillance of *NuCal*. Each had been shot once in the head, execution style. The man was carrying one of my business cards.

The arson investigators had determined that the bomb had detonated in a back room of *NuCal.* They described that back room as a "film lab." Two of the head-shot women had been employees of *NuCal,* which supposedly dealt only in costume design, but one of those victims also worked as a respected free-lance film editor.

Edgar's theory had me implicated right up to just short of planting the bombs and pulling the triggers. He even made mention of my past experience with explosives when I was at LAPD, suggesting I could have made the bombs.

He also had a clincher. Supposedly he had an anonymous tip that I had been paid fifty thousand dollars in cash by Bernard Wiseman to help him fake his own death.

The motive: a scandal brewing at *United Talents* and Wiseman's fear of a coming indictment on criminal charges. No substantiation but it made a good enough story to string me out and give County a focus of public interest in the case.

It mattered not a damn that the officers dispatched to arrest me had found me unconscious and bleeding on my office floor. Edgar did not even wish to discuss it, except for a wise comment about thieves falling out. He was trying to provoke me into attacking him, and maybe I would have if I'd been myself. I was just too sick to rise to his bait. I think I had a mild concussion, the man at the trauma center apparently didn't bother to check it out. He put a butterfly on my lacerated scalp and sent me, he thought, off to jail.

Well, I really wasn't willing to go to jail, nor sick

enough to let Edgar have his way with me. And I did have some resources. I have never liked to think of friends in just those terms, but sometimes you're reminded. Mark Shapiro is a friend. He is also one of the best criminal lawyers in the area and he isn't in it for the money. Mark is about forty years old, a displaced New Yorker who came West for his bar exams after flunking twice back East. He says that the New York bar was rigged against him and that he would never have been admitted to it. I don't know why. I do know that "passing the bar"—any bar—is not necessarily a matter of simply passing the tests. Mark says it's no more than a method for controlling the numbers in the club. That may be true in some areas. Anyone who can survive the rigors of a decent law school shouldn't have that much trouble passing the bar, with appropriate cramming.

Whatever, Mark Shapiro is one smart fellow. He is also a friend and sometime employer. He has hired me to help him on several criminal cases. Law and hockey were his only passions that I'd ever discovered. You might think that the fellow is something of a nerd, unless you'd seen him in a courtroom or at a hockey game. He has a warrior's heart in both arenas, and I'd quickly learned to respect him in any arena.

He was waiting for me downtown. Nobody said so but I suspected that Forta had tipped him. I do know that I was glad to see him there when they brought me in. He hand-held me through all the ignominious formalities, and we walked out the door at nine o'clock on the dot. I was free on my own "recognizance pending an arraignment not yet scheduled." Better yet, my license was intact "pending further developments." All of which was a tribute to Shapiro's aggressive skills and warrior heart. Even though the whole case against me, to that point, was purely circumstantial, without a good, combative lawyer at my side, Edgar would have locked me up and hidden the keys at least until an arraignment hearing.

When I was released, we went outside and stood on the steps to talk for a moment. "I can't believe those guys, trying to pull that kind of crap on you, Joe. Who the hell do they think we are?"

I caught that "we" and appreciated it.

"I mean, with your exemplary police record, to come up with cockamamie charges like those."

"Save it for the judge, pal, we'll probably need it. Speaking of which—you must know that for all practical purposes you're defending an indigent. You'll probably have to take it out in trade, so you'd better do it quick while I still have a license."

"They'll play hell getting your license, Joe."

A man's friends are his greatest treasures, especially for a man like me. I told him that and it embarrassed him. He covered it by telling me, "Be very careful, Joe. This matter is drawing a lot of press. A lot of press automatically translates to heavy politics, and that translates to pressure on everyone to look their best. That includes you, my friend, so be forewarned. I know you like to cut corners here and there. I'm saying you can't do that now, at least until we've disposed of these cockamamie charges. Don't give them any new ammunition."

I promised to behave myself, we set up a meeting for the next afternoon, he went his way and I mine, back inside. Forta was skulking about the lobby, waiting for me. We went to the snack bar and got some coffee, found a table in an empty corner and he told me even before we sat down: "I'm not going to compromise my position, Joe, so be careful what you tell me. There's a lot of heat on. We're friends, but let's not test that friendship in this kind of heat."

I said, "Hadn't planned to tell you a damned thing, friend. Hoping you'd have something to tell me. What about Melissa Franklin?"

"What about her?"

"You took my statement. What were the signs when you got to my office?"

"No signs at all. Your car was parked outside, the engine was still warm, your office was open and you were lying on the floor in your own blood. No signs of forced entry or other disturbance of any kind. I think the woman set you up, Joe, from what you gave us. Must have had someone waiting for you inside."

"Or possibly she was posted as a lookout and I surprised, as you say, a burglary in progress."

"Possibly. What would they be looking for?"

"Something connected to my job for Wiseman. Why did Edgar hand me over?"

"You know Edgar. He'd give up his mother to break this case. Enough to get some headlines, anyway. Wait'll you see the morning papers. He had the reporters in before I got you booked."

"What do you have on Melissa Franklin?"

"Some mystery there. The DMV record is confused. She's had two name changes since the original driver's license was issued six years ago." He got out a small spiral notebook, flipped it open, consulted it. "Originally surrendered a Wisconsin permit and was licensed in California as Melissa Ann Nordstrom.

Married less than a year later, name changed to Moore. Two years ago . . ."

He took a short breath. "Well, well . . ."

I said, "Moore, huh?"

He repeated, "Well, well."

"Albert and Melissa . . ."

"Don't rub it in."

"Which means you haven't cross-checked the vital statistics."

"Too busy," he said, "making a lame collar on a friend of mine."

"Level with me, then, how lame is that collar?"

"You should know."

"I know how easy it is to stretch the facts into a noose," I said. "I'd just like to know how much stretch there is."

"Enough so that you shouldn't get cocky about it," was all he would tell me.

"Run the make on Albert and Melissa," I suggested. "Zero in on that guy and learn all you can about past and present ties to Melissa Franklin. Get it to me as quick as you can, please. If you can't run me down leave the message on my machine."

"Okay, I guess I can do that."

"It'll make up for the collar."

"Or draw it tighter."

"I'll run that risk. Just feed me what you can feed me, Ken. I swear on whoever's grave you want I'm clean."

"If you're holding out on me, Joe . . ."

I copied the information on Melissa Franklin from Forta's notebook while he looked around the room, then I got up and walked away.

He called after me, "Watch it, asshole."

Between us I *think* he meant it as a term of affection.

Later it wouldn't matter. I would never see him alive again.

CHAPTER SEVEN

I was adrift in town at night without a car. I looked like a derelict and felt like one. I was feeling a bit sorry for myself too, like a kicked dog. I called a friend, Nancy Parker—she has a place up near Griffith Park—and requested sanctuary. She came and got me and took me to her place, fed and bathed me and put me to bed with a massage. I fell asleep while she was working on me and woke up alone in the house next morning.

There's nothing romantic between us—nothing serious—we're friends and sometimes one provides extra comfort for the other when the need is there. Nancy is an independent casting director and lives the busy life. She's pretty, smart, a woman who likes to take care of herself. We respect each other. I guess that's our big suit.

She'd washed my shirt and underwear, sponged and pressed my suit, had coffee waiting to be plugged in and breakfast in the microwave ready for a quick warming. She'd also left me a note of one word: *Fear.*

I didn't connect it right away but it came to me over breakfast. I had been feeling pretty lousy the night before and I guess a little down on everything, and I'd asked her a purely rhetorical question: "What the hell's going on with the human race, anyway?"

Sometimes you can get the feeling nothing good is going down—like dog eat dog, survival of the fittest, to hell with you, hooray for me. You get a lot of that in police work. *Fear* apparently was Nancy's answer to the question without an answer. Fear of what? Dying? Pain? Not being loved? What?

Okay, what *fear* was driving this case?

One strong enough to kill and maim and destroy, for sure.

I guess that's what life is all about, after all. For sure it is what the human race is all about. We left the only real sanctuary behind at Eden. Now we are driven by the two great opposites, fear and love.

It was fear of the unknown that was driving me when I left Nancy's place that morning and returned to the war zone. The rubble that had once been *NuCal Designs* was roped off and secured as a "crime scene." An arson team was at work back near the alleyway and a uniformed cop stood vigil up-front. "Anything new?" I asked the sentry.

He gave me a look, nothing more, so I handed him my ID wallet. He looked it over and gave it back, unimpressed. "It's still secured. If you're working for the insurance companies you'll have to route through Lieutenant Johnson of the homicide division."

"Thanks, but I'm not. I was involved in an investi-

gation before the bombing and I've been cooperating
with Johnson's investigation. Just wanted to see it for
myself. Pretty grim scene, isn't it?"

"Sure is." He shuffled about for a moment, then told
me, "I never met a private detective. It's not like on
television, huh. What kind of investigation?"

I shrugged. "Nothing is like on television, pal."

"Right," he said. "What kind of . . . ?"

"Routine surveillance," I told him. "Had a video
eye on the place the whole day of the bombing, right
up until about an hour before."

"Yeah? Front and back?"

I made a sad face and told him, "Front only. That's
all the client wanted."

"Always the way, isn't it. With all the action maybe
going the other way."

"Yeah," I said, in my best television imitation, and
went on my way.

You get these blind spots, you know, even as a cop
and sometimes especially as a cop. I had known all
along that there was a rear entrance to that building—that is, from the moment I began preparing the
actual surveillance. First thing I noted. But then I
was looking at the job through the eyes of my client,
and it had been clear to me that his eyes were interested in the customer-entrance at the front of the
building. So that's where I had fixed my interest,
hadn't given another thought to that alleyway entrance, not even after the talk about a "film lab" in
the back room.

So now I was thinking about it, and the wide-eyed
cop's reference to it. I went to a sidewalk phone
booth, tried to contact Abe Johnson, was told he was
in a meeting and would probably be tied up there all

morning. A guy panhandled me for a quarter while I was standing there at the telephone, and I idly watched him disappear into a liquor store at the corner. Two of his world had died recently and nearby . . . I followed him into the liquor store, a scudsy hole whose specialties were half-pint liquors and cheap wine.

My subject was at the counter and going through a handful of coins to pay for a bottle of Ripple when I got in there. I grabbed a bottle of the same and stood behind him to pay for it, then I followed him outside with my identical brown bag and let him lead me on a beeline toward his own idea of sanctuary.

These are the non-people of out society, you know, most of the time totally invisible to the rest of us until they display themselves in a way that disturbs our own sense of comfort. But I discovered a long time ago that the street people have their own community and values. Some can wax quite philosophical on their views, if you're willing to listen, and some of those can sometimes make a lot of sense.

I really was not looking for any of that. I cultivated the guy because I know the ways of these people and understand their community. Two of that local community had died recently and very close by. I was just wondering if anything useful could be learned in that connection.

We ended up in a cardboard crate beside a trash bin in an alley just one block over from the blast zone, and we clinked our bottles together as we settled down to a serious contemplation of life and its incomprehensible vicissitudes. His name was George, he was about fifty, and he'd found the truth about all of it.

"We're not s'posed to know," he gravely informed me. "That's what it all means. Not s'posed to know."

"Right," I agreed.

"Soon as you know, you die."

I said, "Oh."

"Sure. Bein' alive is not knowin' why you're alive. Soon's you find out, you die. S'what death is, knowin' it all. See? You ready for that?"

I said, "Not me."

He said, "Me neither. So here's to not knowin'." We clinked bottles again. "Celebrate, celebrate. That's the secret."

I said, "Right. How 'bout your buddies, though? I mean the fire the other night. Let's celebrate for them."

Again we brought the bottles together.

George said, "You just never know, anymore."

I reminded him, " 'Til we die."

"That, too. But you don't even know what's safe anymore. I told 'em."

"What'd you tell 'em, George?"

"Told 'em that place was too busy. You know. Too much out the back door. You know what that means."

I said, "Sure. The front is the back and back is the front. How do you know which is which?"

"Exactly," George replied, and we drank a toast to that. "All hours of the day and night," he added. "I told Willie. I told 'im. 'You're gonna catch a bullet out there some night, Willie. You better find another place to live.' He wouldn't listen."

We clinked and drank to Willie and his sudden gift of knowledge.

I put my bottle down between George's legs and asked him to watch it for me, then I walked away from that cardboard sanctuary without looking back, but I thought about it for a long time afterward. We look at the street people and feel superior, and in that superiority we pity them and their screwloose approach to life. Are there larger beings somewhere who occasionally pierce our veils of invisibility and then feel the same way about us and all of our proud postures?

I had not actually drunk any of the Ripple but I was sure that it would not go to waste.

The bottle was the real sanctuary for people like George, the only one worth pursuing. I hoped he would find comfort there. Because he'd really helped me a lot. I was finally beginning to develop my own theory of the case.

A theory about myself, too, and my own postures.

And I think I'd decided that there are no real sanctuaries, not anywhere or for anybody . . . this side of the grave. I was thinking that George had not been too far off the mark, at that—especially for those of us who think of knowledge and position as some sort of sanctuary from growth, which is just another word for life.

That was my Ripple revelation.

Only the dead find sanctuary.

CHAPTER EIGHT

I had lunch with a tense and fidgety Abe Johnson and found him a bit cool, almost distant with me, especially early on. That was understandable. He did not give me much over lunch, but he did know that I'd been charged at County and seemed to want my version of it, which I gave him.

I told him I thought Edgar was shooting from the hip and hoping for a lucky strike.

"Don't count on that," Abe said. "They've got good cops over there. You should know. Don't sell them short. Matter of fact, we're reevaluating all the evidence ourselves. Taking a fresh look at all of it, including your input—and frankly, Joe, none of it seems to hang together. This is a messy case. None of the pieces seem to fit together, especially not with your pieces."

I had to wonder what Abe knew that he was not sharing with me. "If it's all that messy, then I'd guess someone set it up that way. You should be wondering why, and while you're doing that you should keep remembering who the patsy is. If I was a criminal part of it, don't you think I'd know how to cover myself better than that?"

"That's the way I've been trying to look at it."

"I'm getting the strong feeling I was set up coming in. Why? For what? Why make me a fall guy to a conspiracy? What would that buy anybody?"

"That's part of what we're wondering—"

"Well, please keep on wondering. And while you're at it, wonder about Melissa Franklin too. I'm not sure that she's the one I saw in the limo. I'm not sure that Wiseman is the Albert Moore who hired me. I'm not sure that the real Albert Moore was driving that limo, and I'm not sure that the real Melissa Franklin was in that limo moments before it destructed or that she was in my office yesterday when I got sapped from behind. I'm not sure, period."

Johnson said, "So you see our problem. Very messy, too many possibilities. And what's frying the whole thing now—"

"The executions?"

"Right. You took pictures of fourteen people outside *NuCal* before the bombing, ostensibly to identify a disloyal employee at *United Talents.* From one point of view that set the whole chain of events in motion—beginning with the bombing of the building and continuing on to the execution-style slaying of four of the people you photographed. We're trying to identify and warn the others, just in case any more have been marked, but there's been no luck there. Not yet. We're probably going to have to put it on the air and request those people to come forward and identify themselves."

"Sounds reasonable."

"Unless some are criminally tainted. There's evidence to suggest that *NuCal Designs* was a front for illegal activities in the back room."

"The film lab?"

"Yeah. More than that, looks like they were manufacturing video cassettes back there too. We're figuring it as a possible pirate operation. With Wiseman in the picture—and in light of what he told you when he hired you—we're thinking it could have involved a ripoff of UT's big hits using the film from their own vaults. If Wiseman had tumbled to something like that . . ."

By the look on his face, his stops and starts, it was clear that Johnson was having trouble buying his theories. "Doesn't ring, though, does it. Why would a man in Wiseman's position, and stuck in a wheelchair, want to play it that way? These big studios have their own security setups. Why didn't he just turn it over to his security honcho or to the cops?"

Johnson sighed. "Yeah. Unless the rumors are true."

"What rumors?"

"That Wiseman was very kinky himself and that a faction at UT has been trying to expose him."

"You want to tell me more about that?"

"Not 'til I know more about it myself."

Over coffee, I reminded him: "Wiseman or Moore, or whoever paid me the thirteen hundred, hinted that he was trying to set up a disinformation game. Maybe that was the one true thing he said to me."

"So what does that buy?"

"A confusion of the circumstances," I said. "If the guy was not being straight with me, then the whole setup could have been for the purpose of disinformation—confusion. That would be the only reason I'm in it. Just because it made no sense. Helter-skelter. The only other reasoning that makes sense to me is to take it back to square one and say that an honest man came to me with an honest problem and I was trying to help him solve it."

Abe provided a sour smile. "That would solve your problem, wouldn't it. But as I've said, the pieces don't match. In that scenario how do we account for the four murders since the bombings?"

"Two games in play? Wiseman, or whoever, came to me to help set up the one game. But he was too late. While he was trying to get his play going, the other game overtook him and knocked him out of play."

"Wiseman or whoever . . ."

"Yes. Someone came to me and said that he was being ripped off. He wanted information that would help him to fight back. Before he could use the information I provided he was taken out of play. The others would have been killed whether or not I'd been out there taking pictures. Which leaves me clean. I performed a proper service for a proper client. I just happened to get caught in the crossfire."

"Makes some sense," Johnson said. "And that's the way I've been trying to read it."

"So why isn't County reading it that way?"

"It's more intriguing the other way," he said. "I had a meeting this morning with the department brass and two councilmen. Everyone's upset by the press attention. No one, surprise, surprise, wants to come out with egg on the face. The political implications . . . well, you know, there are a lot of aspirations in various quarters that reach a way beyond this city. Nobody wants to look like a fool, Joe. And this case already has caught the attention of the whole country. This might have to be the last friendly meeting between you and me, so—"

"Don't you dump on me, Abe."

"You must realize why I've bent so far backward to avoid that very thing, Joe."

I tried to read that bland cop-face. So okay, he'd brought it up. "How is she?" I asked him.

"She's fine," he said quietly. "No hard feelings toward you, for what it's worth."

"That's nice. But there was no reason for hard feelings either way. We made a mistake. We corrected it. It was never a happy marriage, Abe. I hope she's happy now."

"She is, we are. Two kids. One black and one white."

"Fair enough," I said. "Police colors."

He turned serious. "I'll do what I can for you, Joe, but you should know that there are limits. If I see you going down, you have to know that I intend to stand clear. Too much to lose. I'm not like you, I've got—"

"I know." I put down ten bucks to cover my part of the check, stood up. "You're already too close, Abe." I stuck out my hand. "Thanks for trying."

I received an envelope instead of a handshake—an envelope and a wink. I put the envelope in a pocket and sent the wink back to him as I stepped away.

He said, "Take care."

I waved without looking back and went on out.

Nice guy, and that was my opinion even before I opened the envelope.

I had a complete abstract of Abe Johnson's investigation—names and addresses of all the victims, places of employment, a thumbnail history of Wiseman and his record at *United Talents,* of Moore and Melissa Franklin—plus a set of 35mm negatives processed from my videotape.

I went into a one-hour photo shop and ordered four-by-five-inch prints of the fourteen negatives, then studied the abstract while waiting for the prints. There was some interesting stuff. Wiseman had a wife living in San Marino; they'd been legally separated for two years and she'd recently filed for divorce. Moore had come to *United Talents* with Wiseman and had been married to Melissa Franklin at the time. Melissa had divorced Moore less than a year later and immediately married a screenwriter named Charles Franklin—status of that marriage not clear.

It was beginning to sound like a soap.

The photo guy was very upset over his prints. They were a bit fuzzy, and he complained about marks on some of the negatives that carried over onto the prints. I told him it was fine, paid him and got out of there.

The "marks" were actually etchings that had been placed on four of the negatives by technicians at the police lab, identification codes for the latest four victims. They were covered in the abstract.

I could understand why Abe Johnson had been so edgy during our luncheon.

The fuse was still burning.

There could be ten more victims before the thing had run its course. And nobody even knew why the others had died.

I decided it was about time someone found out why.

That fuse was burning toward me too.

It was time to stop feeling like a victim and start acting like a cop. I intended to do exactly that.

CHAPTER NINE

I kept my appointment with Mark Shapiro and we spent ten minutes discussing the case in his office, then he volunteered to drive me home and I took him up on it. Not that I intended to go home but I needed my car. To be afoot in the L. A. area is to be stranded. We played bumper-cars along the San Bernardino Freeway. Mark drives like most New Yorkers—with fury and faith in a higher power—it was not a restful trip. We got to my office in record time and it was just past three when Mark screeched out of the parking lot and left me debating with myself about my next move.

I decided to go inside and check the office for signs. Nothing—nothing on the answer machine, nothing out of place. I don't know what I'd hoped to find.

On impulse I went next door to the beauty salon for a chat with the owner, a fiftyish woman named Molly who is a terrible advertisement for her business, but any meet with her is good for smiles and excellent coffee.

She showed me a brightly expectant face and raised a coffee cup as I walked in. Several customers were receiving the usual attentions from beauticians in booths along the wall. I always get uncomfortable looks from the chair-bound patrons when I go in there, sort of like what you'd expect from an intrusion into a ladies' room. I followed Molly to a little alcove in the rear where she served up a fresh brew and the standard running gag. "You look like hell, Joe."

"Thanks. So do you."

"So let's go to your place and console each other."

I faked appropriate disappointment, as usual, as I replied, "Can't. I'm on a case."

One day I'm going to take her up on that, just to determine if she's faking it too.

"You're always on a case," she replied tartly. "I saw her yesterday. What's she got that I don't have?— other than youth, beauty and wealth?"

Exactly why I came in. Molly sees a lot from behind her cash register.

"Tall blond girl?"

"Driving a fancy car, yes. Was that a Jaguar?"

"Uh huh."

"Don't be so coy. The cops already asked me about it.

"When was that?"

"This morning. Plainclothes cops. They asked a lot of questions."

"About me?"

"No, about Santa Claus, dummy. Don't worry, I told them you're great in bed."

"Guess I'll have to prove it now, huh?"

"Any time you feel like you can, Tiger."

We laughed and lit cigarettes. It was our usual banter. I think she's all talk. Molly has been married to the same man for thirty years. If her usual appearance is any guide, she lost real interest in sex long ago but has fun talking about it.

I told her, "I'm in some trouble, Molly. For real. I need—"

"Is it that bombing? I knew it! That was the same damned limousine, wasn't it!"

"You saw that too, huh?"

"Sure I saw it. Everyone in this complex saw it. Was that really Bernie Wisemsn?"

"Looks that way, yeah," I replied. "I was hired to do some routine work for the guy. Now they're trying to implicate me in a string of murders."

"That's crazy!" Molly said angrily. "You send those guys back around here to talk to me again! I'll tell them!"

"What did you tell them before?"

"Not much. Didn't know much to tell. They asked about the blond, the car she was driving. I told them what I knew. Was that wrong?"

"Course it wasn't wrong. What did you know to tell them?"

"Well . . . she sat out there for about an hour— waiting for you, I guess. I thought at first maybe she was waiting to pick up one of my customers. We had a rush yesterday, the place was full all day. I asked around after about an hour, but nobody claimed her. I didn't see you arrive, guess I was looking the other way when you came in, or maybe I was busy in the back. I just know I looked out and saw your car parked beside hers and both were empty. Sorry."

"Did you see her leave?"

"*Heard* her leave. That car scream out of here like the devil was chasing it. I just caught a glimpse as it tore past. Figured you'd broken her heart, you devil."

"How long was that after you saw my car?"

"Oh . . . just a few minutes, I guess. Short time after."

"Could you tell if anyone besides the blond was in that car?"

"Not even her, Joe. It was just a flash past the window."

"See anything else of interest?"

"No. I can't think of anything else."

"Anyone hanging around my office? Anything unusual in the parking lot?"

"No."

"Nobody else coming or going."

"No. I locked up at six. Your car was still out there and the lights were on in the office. I didn't see anything unusual."

I showed her the bald spot and butterfly bandage on my scalp and told her, "Someone sapped me while that blond was in my office. I must have been lying in there unconscious when you loked up and went home. You can't remember *any*thing unusual or out of focus or . . ."

"Just that fancy car tearing out of here. Sorry, Joe. I'm going to have to start keeping tabs on you, Tiger. Sounds like you need a keeper."

"So do you," I said, resuming the gag and fingering a lock of her hair. "When's the last time you washed your hair?"

"Same time you aired out your jockeys," she fired back. "Did you get raped in jail, lover?"

I asked, "How'd you know I'd been to jail?"

She leaned over and flipped a newspaper from the rack. Big black headlines proclaimed: LOCAL PI CHARGED IN L.A. BOMBING.

I told her, "You had me coming in, didn't you."

She told me, "I wish."

I couldn't tell if the gag was still running or not.

So I thanked my interesting neighbor and got out of there.

I hadn't learned a hell of a lot in a positive sense, but sometimes there is knowledge from a negative sense. And I decided that I'd better go home and look for signs there.

I live only about ten minutes from the office, north into the foothills of the San Gabriel mountains. It's a developed area with a great view onto the entire valley and all its communities, zoned for horses and peopled by folks who like same. I don't, but I like the stretch between the houses so I put up with the flies as a small penalty to pay for the luxury of uncluttered space. My home is my only true luxury, which means that I can't afford it but I'm damned if I'll live any other way and I'm willing to sacrifice in other areas of lifestyle.

Well, I do have one other luxury, but it's business-connected so really doesn't qualify. It's the van I mentioned earlier. It's outfitted for business but easily convertible for camping. If the IRS is listening, don't worry: I pro-rate it out as a business expense, even though I have yet to use it for any other purpose. I consider it a business luxury because I don't use it that often. Usually I drive the old Cadillac, a fully paid for Eldorado built before the EPA standards, three damned tons of beautiful, gas-guzzling decadence. I love it, so maybe it's a minor luxury too when it comes time for the monthly gas bills. I get triple the mileage from the van, and it sits in the garage most of the time.

So anyway I was driving the Cad. And I decided I needed to go home and scout for signs.

Signs of what? I didn't know what. Maybe I was just feeling a bit paranoid, maybe something precognitive was growling around in the bowels of the mind—I didn't know. I just knew that I should go home and check it out.

On the way, I decided that I should clean up and change clothes while I was there, maybe have a bite to eat to fortify the evening—and that leapt me to the realization that I had not been home for a couple of days and the pantry was probably bare. So I stopped at a supermarket along the way and picked up a few items, got home about four o'clock with my sack of groceries.

I have to confess that I'm a little vain about my home. Maybe it's because I never had one to take much pride in until I was a teen-ager, I don't know. My dad died when I was little and my mother never got over it. All that was good in her sort of died with him, I think. I don't blame her; I can very unemotionally state that my mother was a tramp in all my memories of her—and most of what I feel in that connection is pity, not bitterness.

I spent my teen years in a foster home, and it was the tender influences of that home that led me into police work. I've never been anything but a cop, never aspired to anything else. But I always had the greatest reverence for a nice home, and I am proud to say that I have one of those now. I also have acreage, and I like gardening—do all my own.

Neighbors I don't have, not close neighbors. We like it that way in the hills, respect one another's privacy, and the terrain contributes to it nicely.

I mention all this as background for the next development in the case.

I arrive home at four o'clock to find a strange car parked in my driveway. It is an unmarked police car, the type used by the County of Los Angeles. The window on the driver's side is down and a police radio mutters at low volume.

The front door to my palace stands ajar.

Just inside, on a small foyer table, lies a search warrant with my name and address on it.

In the hallway leading to my bedroom-study I find a cold corpse lying face down in coagulated blood. I don't recognize the face, but his ID, still clutched between stiff fingers, tells me that he was Detective Herman Rodriguez of the sheriff's San Gabriel division.

In my study, slumped over my desk, I find a second corpse.

I did not need the ID for this one.

This one is my old pal and confidant, Ken Forta.

And now Joe Copp was really on fire.

CHAPTER TEN

Both men had been shot once in the chest and apparently the shooter or shooters knew how to do it right the first time. Death had come quickly, probably without warning. Neither had drawn his weapon. Rodriguez seemed to have been presenting his ID when he got it. In trying to reconstruct, I knew either there had to be two shooters firing near-simultaneously or one shooter using a silenced weapon, because the two officers had died with no evidence of struggle or even self-defense, and within twenty paces of each other.

Either someone had been waiting for me when the officers came, or someone had been surprised by their arrival during a burglary. It read the same either way. So . . . had someone let them in?—someone who would not arouse particular suspicion by being there?—or had someone hidden when the cops arrived, then came out during the search to blast clear and get away?

Forta had been sitting at my desk when he got it. He had produced a search warrant and left it prominently displayed in the entryway. Rodriguez was surprised in the hallway, ID in hand. Both had been dead for some time. Molly had told me that she'd been visited by "plainclothes cops" that morning. Same cops? Had they then come up only to search my house?

There was no evidence of a search by anyone. Everything seemed to be in place.

I did not call it in and I did not hang around. Dead is dead, I could do nothing for them now. I could do something for myself, though. I left everything exactly the way I'd found it, even the front door ajar, and I got away from there, groceries and all.

Some crazy son of a bitch was running wild, killing wild, and I had the sick feeling that somehow I'd helped launch this thing. I could do nothing about that now—but for sure I could try to *stop* it.

I've never been able to take death casually, not any death anywhere for any reason, not even death in bed from old age. A police psychologist once tried to tell me that was because I feared death so much for myself, but that's a crock. I think it's because I learned at an early age and through personal experience that death is always a personal loss to everyone left alive. Today we take death too casually. Murder is no longer a heinous crime. In this state now there even has to be "special circumstances" before a prosecutor can request for the death penalty.

But murder is a heinous crime because it takes something irreplaceable from all of us, whether or not we know the victim. Murder touches us all in some fine way. Ken Forta is no longer around to pull your baby from a burning building or to stop a drunk driver twenty seconds before he would've slammed into a school bus carrying your kids and all your neighbor's kids. He isn't here now to coach a Pop Warner team or to take a brotherly interest in screwed-up teen-agers or to turn a street gang onto a Toys for Tots drive next Christmas.

It touches us all, pal, each of us and all of us in many fine ways. We're all in this thing together and the loss is real for all of us when any of us takes the tumble. Try to remember that the next time you have to wait a couple of minutes at an intersection for a funeral procession; instead of impatience, try a little grief for a stranger whose death has diminished you.

Of course I was thinking in no such terms at the moment. I was just mad as hell and scared as hell ... I came down out of the hills and onto the Foothills Freeway, cruising west and starting to think like a cop again with Abe Johnson's abstract open on the seat beside me. San Marino leapt to my eye as the home of Justine Wiseman and because it was just a few minutes down the pike. It's one of the more affluent areas, sort of a Beverly Hills East with extensive neighborhoods of stately homes and million-dollar estates. Some of the movie people live out there. It was on my way and I was in rush-hour traffic—which isn't all that different anymore from midnight traffic or midmorning traffic; it's always bumper-to-bumper; there's just more stop-and-go during rush-hour—so I got off the freeway at Huntington and cruised past Santa Anita and on to San Marino. The surface routes were not much clearer than the freeway, but at least there's some justification for stop-and-go there so it doesn't affect my blood pressure as much.

It was about five o'clock when I found the Wiseman residence—not Bernard's anymore but still Justine's. He'd moved to Bel Air when they separated, poor guy, had to give up one stately mansion and start all over in another—the American Dream in Southern California, his-and-hers mansions.

This one was no slouch by any standards, not even Bel Air's. It gives me a shiver to even try to guess the current market value of such digs. I pulled the old Cad onto the circular drive and left it under the canopy at the front door behind a gleaming Mercedes SL. A uniformed Chicano maid answered my ring, a lovely young woman with glowing dark eyes that dulled a bit at the sight of my ID. Her English probably was not up to the fine distinction between public and private badges, so I didn't try to draw it.

She left me standing in the marbled foyer amid exotic potted trees and museum-quality objets d'art while she went to fetch the lady of the house.

I did a double-take when that one arrived, heart pounding between takes, because Justine Wiseman was a tall, tanned California-vintage blonde who could double in long shots for Melissa Franklin. Up close the difference was more obvious. This one seemed a couple of years older and didn't have the same thing in the eyes, but she had it all everywhere else. I would not have evicted her from my hot-tub club. She wore workout tights and legwarmers, a towel draped across the shoulders, much irritation in the face.

"How many times do I have to go through this?" she said.

"How many so far?"

"Two policemen were here yesterday and another two today. Can't you people ever get it *right?*"

"It's a big case."

"Well, what is it this time?"

I produced the photographs and handed them to her.

"I've already looked at these."

"Please look again. For me. And look closer this time. Tell me who you see."

She bestowed a sudden smile. "Oh, I see. The kids couldn't handle the job, so the boss had to come back to handle this difficult lady."

"Something like that. Look, cops don't work in a vacuum and we're not magicians. We need help. We're asking for yours. And . . . you do have a vested interest in all this."

"Cut the crap, cop. I have no interest whatever. If the son of a bitch is dead, that's too bad for some but it's okay with me. Don't look for tears in my eyes. He used me and left me. I'm supposed to wear black and weep over his grave? Not me. Screw him. And you too. Now get out of here and leave me alone."

She handed the pictures over and flounced away.

I called after her, "Screw you too, lady."

She halted and turned around with a smile; said, in a friendlier tone, "Well I've got a live one here."

"Too damned close to a dead one, pal. I just left two who died in my place. That brings the body count to thirteen. For what? Who's next? You?"

"You think . . . ?"

"Haven't you? Does your mind work as fast as your jaw?"

She was wearing a small smile now. "You're not supposed to talk to me like that."

"Works both ways."

"What do you want to know?"

"Status of your marriage, for starters."

"Dead. He was what they call a man of the world, he'd already screwed up three previous marriages. I was a nineteen-year-old kid—trusting, dumb as hell. He signed me to a marriage contract so he could dump me cheap when something better came along. My lawyers have been working on that. We figured we were ready to face his lawyers in court. So now he's dead and we won't have to do that, will we? Does that make me a suspect? Well forget it, because now we have to sue his estate, all the previous wives and God knows how many kids who might crawl out of the woodwork. Am I sad he's dead? Hell, no. I'm madder'n hell, though, and I could kill the son of a bitch that did it to him and complicated my life."

"Let the state do it for you," I suggested. "Help us do it for you."

"What else do you want?"

"Tell me about Albert Moore."

"Albert is a geek."

I waited.

"A geek is a sideshow freak who eats live chickens. Albert would eat live chickens if he thought it would please Bernard. If I hadn't known better for sure, I'd have suspected, like they say, an unnatural attraction between the two."

"I see. But you know better for sure."

"Unless they're both bi, yes."

"Okay. Let's try another. Melissa Moore Franklin."

Mrs. Wiseman laughed and retreated a couple of paces. "Melissa Moore rhymes with whore, and that is what she is for sure."

I wondered what I was getting here. "A whore for sure?"

"Melissa Moore—or Franklin or whatever she calls herself these days—is a whore for sure. Haven't you seen her old movies?"

"Which are those?"

"Cinderella Balls?, Passion's Pucker? She's sucked and fucked every porno stud in town. Cops don't watch porn like other natural men?"

Well, you can see, I had a live one too.

She invited me into the gym for tea and I took her up on it.

I had a live one, yes. And I began to wonder how long I could keep her that way.

CHAPTER ELEVEN

I loved and hated the lady. She could be bitchy but also frank and witty. Everything was right up-front. She said what came to mind, never picked at words.

She'd been married to Wiseman for thirteen years, which made her thirty-two now. If she'd ever been nineteen and dumb, no one would ever guess it. Her husband had become disabled after their separation, the result of a freak horseback accident in Mexico while he was down there with one of his location units—some sort of spinal damage. Says she went down to visit him in the Mexican hospital and he ordered her out. The injury had done nothing to improve his character—and it was shortly after his return to L.A. that he took up with Melissa, who just months earlier had married the screenwriter Charles Franklin.

I wondered about his paralysis and his ability to

work out with Melissa. Justine assured me that he would find a way; she was just as sure that Melissa would find something to suffice in her bag of tricks.

I also wondered about Albert and how he might have felt about chauffeuring around his ex-wife with his boss.

"He did more than chauffeur," Justine informed me. "He also bathed him, put him to bed, and probably shook his dick when he peed. So maybe Albert helped out in bed too. I told you, he would eat live chickens for Bernard. What does an ex-wife have to do with anything? My God, if he could stand the porno studs, what couldn't he stand?"

"Were they married while she was doing that?"

"Not to hear them tell it, but as far as I know she's still doing it. How old do you have to get to disqualify as a starlet?"

"How old is she?"

"Twenty-eight going on eighty, depending on which part of the anatomy you're wondering about. If you figure roughly six inches to the stroke and a hundred strokes to an encounter . . . that's right about fifty feet of cock per orgasm. About a hundred of those gets you a mile. She's got to have at least fifty cock-miles on her."

She gave that to me with an absolutely straight face.

I wanted to talk some more about her husband but Justine was itching to get out of her tights and into the shower. The "gym" was a room about twenty-by-fifty feet with Nautilus equipment and an aerobics mat, massage table, a corner lounge with overstuffed couches and large-screen TV. It connected to her bedroom via a huge bath with a circular sunken tub, island shower, another massage table . . .

"There's room for two in the shower," she told me, and casually stripped off the tights as I sat there.

I said weakly, stupidly, "Thanks, I had mine Saturday."

She shrugged, went into the bathroom, kept on talking to me through the open doorway while she showered. Wasn't much of a conversation because she couldn't hear me over the shower noise and I wasn't about to get any closer.

Under almost any other circumstances I can think of I would have *carried* that lady into her shower and carefully scrubbed every inch of her. Probably I would have contributed to her cock-miles.

But this wasn't James Bond time. I was burning, true, but not with sexual passion . . .

Later I was glad I'd kept perspectives intact. Because this big Viking of a woman came in shortly thereafter and began preparing the massage table—chiseled body, muscled thighs, looking as though she could wring you dry and squeeze the life out of you.

She looked at me. "Shall I put the tables together?"

"Thanks, I can't stay."

No way was I going to become hamburger patty sandwiched between those two. The Viking was naked as her mistress and breaking out the warm scented oil.

I like to think of it as a strategic retreat.

Actually I fled.

And I could hear the laughter all the way to the front door.

* * *

So what did I have? I knew what it meant in a general sense . . . that sleaze walks the high roads as well as the low, not exactly a big revelation. I worked for ten years behind a public badge in this town and I found most of the surprises during the first couple of years. You haven't met sleaze until you've been exposed to the corporate variety, to Beverly Hills sleaze, high-rise sleaze. These folks have it refined to high art. Wasn't it the rich and powerful who invented the orgy? Nothing wrong with sex, it's what you *do* for it or with it that makes for sleaze.

No, I don't have a Ph.D. in psychology and I've never sat on a philosopher's stone, but I've cruised these streets and I've dealt firsthand with most every variety of human misery. Don't talk theory of plumbing to a guy who's down there with with his hands in it. And don't talk social theory to a cop who lives the reality the profs write about.

What does this have to do with my case?

The aroma of sleaze was strong in my nostrils.

What does it have to do with the case?

Take a good close look at this cast of characters.

CHAPTER TWELVE

Charles Franklin's place was up in the Glendale hills, not swank but no shanty either. He's an urbane man of forty-five, handsome, well set up. I knew at the front door that I did not want to play cute with this one, so I took it straight to him.

"My name is Joe Copp. I'm a private investigator. I've become involved in the Wiseman case."

He took the play away from me right there, stepping back quickly and swinging the door wide to invite me inside with a restrained flourish. "I suppose I've been half expecting you to call," he told me in a voice that sounded a bit like Dick Cavett's. "I knew that Melissa was trying to reach you. Have you spoken with her?"

I resisted the urge to finger the wound on my scalp. "Yes, we talked briefly yesterday. She isn't home, by any chance?"

He said, "Oh, Melissa doesn't live here. I haven't

seen her for days. She did call early yesterday afternoon sounding sort of mysterious and troubled. Of
course I'd already heard the news about Bernie,
so . . ."

He had led me into the interior of what could have
been a plush mountain cabin on a ski slope somewhere. Outside was the usual stucco and brick but
inside was pure Aspen with oversized fireplace, pa-
neled walls, wooden floors with scatter rugs, open
beam ceilings and a picture window that probably
looked all the way to Catalina on a clear day. Nice
place, and it said "bachelor" to me all the way.

He was smoking a pipe as we settled into chairs
near the fireplace. I already knew that this guy had
been a screenwriter for the past twenty years and I'd
been impressed with his list of credits.

I asked him, "How long have you and Melissa been
separated?"

"Oh, we're not separated," he replied quickly.
"That is, not in the conventional sense. It isn't like a
breakup or any of that. We've never lived together."

"Why'd you get married?"

"Marriage of convenience," he said, smiling.

"Okay."

"We're the best of friends."

"Okay."

"How can I help you?"

"I was just with Justine Wiseman. I have her view
of . . . the personalities involved. I'm trying to understand the various relationships."

"Justine can be very direct," he said for the under-
statement of the day.

"I'm hoping you will be too."

"Glad to try. If you're working for Melissa you're

working for me too in a way. What can I tell you?"

I didn't tell him I was not working for Melissa. I said, "Give me a verbal script, set up the characters for me."

He smiled. "A story treatment."

I nodded. "Whatever you call it."

He stared out the window, got up to stand with an arm on the fireplace mantel, worked at his pipe. "Begins with a boy genius, a prodigy who was playing Brahms at the piano before most kids get free of the playpen. Very gifted, and not just in music. He masters music, in fact, to his own satisfaction at least, and has gone on to other interests by the time he's twelve. Shy, reclusive boy—not big on relationships or peer groups or any of that. Then he discovers sex and begins a five-year affair with one of his tutors. He—"

"Male or female tutor?"

"Female. Linguist." He puffed his pipe. "She teaches him all the tongues."

"Five years starting when?"

"Starting at the age of twelve. He's already mastered the usual studies that take a normal kid through high school. Now he's concentrating on economics, languages and sex. He—"

"Who is this kid turning into?"

"Sorry, thought you knew. He's turning into Bernie Wiseman."

"Okay. Please go on."

"He gets a Harvard A.B., economics major, gets bored with the B-school, goes into Wall Street at the age of nineteen. At twenty-five he's CEO of one of the big investment firms and bored again. Now he's playing too hard and gambling too much. There's a small scandal involving an insider trading deal. He's into therapy now and is often seen in the company of . . . cheap-looking women."

"How old now?"

"Still twenty-five. Moves west and is married at twenty-six, divorced and remarried at twenty-eight, again at thirty. The third marriage lasts five years. Meanwhile he's become interested in movies, works briefly in the distribution and marketing end, jumps into production and finance with a small firm that's doing sexploitation pics."

"Porno."

"No. There's a difference. The Russ Meyer sort of thing but without Russ' special touch. These are just . . . you know, drive-in movie stuff. They'd get a PG rating today, and even the thirteen-year-olds would turn up their noses at them. These were grinders. Five days on a sound stage, a day in the cutting room and into the drive-ins next week. He made piles of money, needless to say. But it wrecked his marriage."

"Problems with the casting couch."

"Probably. The problem was always there. Now it was being fed by an inexhaustible supply. The stories are, as they say, legend."

"What stories?"

"In the business, I mean. There was no gossip-column interest in Bernie back then."

"What stories?"

"Oh . . . that he had a different girl for lunch every day in the office . . . a girl comforting him from beneath the desk while he's conducting business . . . similar attention in his car on the freeway, hand jobs beneath the table in fancy restaurants. Those kind of stories."

"The American Dream, eh?"

"I think it was more like a nightmare. I've known the man for ten years, worked with him on six pictures, and that is not the Bernie Wiseman I've known."

"Tell me about that one."

"Kind, generous, compassionate. Those stories have become legend too, by the way. Gifts to repay a kindness, never forgets a favor, never turns on or forgets a friend."

"How about wives?"

"Well, he's just had one since I've known him. Lord knows he tried to get along with Justine. But she can be something of a wildcat."

"How heavy was he into alimony?"

"Pretty heavy, I gather. Joked about it sometimes. Like Carson, just smiled and went on. He's been paying Justine a very generous allowance for the past two years."

I said, "She's still not mourning."

"Well . . . perhaps not—"

"Definitely not."

He restoked his pipe. "Sad. They were very cozy once. I think it came apart for good in Mexico. Did she tell you? He blamed her for the accident with the horse. Very irrational, it was the first time I'd ever seen that in Bernie. He could get fixed on something and you'd have a devil of a time dissuading him, but usually he would yield if you could show him exactly where he was wrong. Not that time. I guess he died blaming her . . . ."

"Are we sure he died?"

Franklin gave me a startled look. "I understood there was no question of that."

"There wasn't much left to identify," I said.

"But the medical records, dental charts . . ."

"Why would he blame Justine? She wasn't even there, was she? Were you there?"

"I was, yes. It was my picture—my script, that is. No, Justine wasn't there. They were already separated. He actually thought she had put a contract out on him. But it was just a freak accident. The horse stumbled and rolled over him."

"So why would he think—?"

"Oh, there was some question about . . . they found brambles or something wedged beneath two of the horses's shoes, enough to make it very touchy at times. The location manager couldn't figure it out because he said that kind of vegetation didn't even grow in that area and they were local horses. Bernie built that inconsistency into a murder plot, and, of course, he blamed Justine."

"Why 'of course'?"

"They were having a bitter wrangle over the divorce settlement. He'd been worried about a loophole in the marriage contract and—"

"What loophole?"

"I don't know all the details. But he seemed to think that she would profit more from his death than from any divorce settlement."

"How much, would you say, was at stake there?"

"Millions. Bernie had a beautiful incentive program at UT. Bonuses, you know, profit sharing. And he's turned nothing but smashes for several years now."

"How did your picture do? The one in Mexico."

He smiled. "That was *Bonaparte's Reprise.*"

Not bad. It had taken a couple of Oscar nomina-

tions and was a top grosser last year. I'd seen it myself
and I rarely go to movies. I asked the writer, "Do you
usually go on location with your pictures?"

"Depends on where the location is. Actually, for
Bonaparte, I'd just flown down with Bernie for a
weekend visit. I did change a couple of scenes while
I was there but . . . well, of course, the accident was
very demoralizing for everyone. Delayed the shooting for a week. I was doing another script for Para-
mount at the time. Bernie was down there for several
months recuperating, but I was there for only a few
days."

"Why did he stay so long? With an injury like that
I'd want to get back home with the best medical attention possible."

"Not Bernie. He really liked it down there and had
confidence in the doctors. And of course he had this
fixation about Justine, a paranoid fixation. I do believe he was afraid to come home until he was on his
feet again."

"And he never got on his feet again."

"Well, but there was some hope for a while, some
possibility that the damaged nerves would mend
themselves, regenerate."

"That never happened."

"Never happened."

I said, "Could we talk a bit about Melissa? Did she
make porno movies?"

"Did Justine tell you that?"

"Yes. Have you seen them?"

"I scripted one of them."

"Why?"

"Why not? It was fun. Pay was lousy but, I admit,
it stirred my fantasies."

I said, "What's to script? I figured those movies were thrown together on the spot."

"Not all. It can be a challenging assignment. The one I did was upscaled a bit, good storyline, some humor."

"But no Oscars."

"Matter of fact, it won a porn award."

We both laughed and then I asked him, "That's when you met Melissa?"

"No, actually Melissa came to me and asked me to do the script. I'd known her since her first week in town. She—"

"This was before her marriage to Albert?"

"Yes, about a year before. She'd done a couple of the adult films when we first met. I didn't know about that at the time. She had an interest in writing and I was doing weekend seminars at UCLA."

"So you got together over the writer's version of the casting couch."

"Oh no, not me," he protested amiably. "I suppose she would have but—"

I asked it pointblank: "Are you gay?"

"As a circumstance of birth, yes. As a choice of lifestyle, no. I haven't slept with a man since I was eighteen. Fallen in love with a few, yes, but I never worked it out through the act."

"Must be difficult."

He smiled, relit his pipe. "Not really. There are other ways of working it out. I have a rich fantasy life. It suffices."

"Ever fantasize about Bernie Wiseman?"

"Of course." He said it easily. "I was in love with Bernie."

"I see."

"Do you?"

"Not really, but it's okay by me if it's okay by you. Maybe I'm out of line to say it, but you don't act like a man whose lover just died."

"We weren't lovers," he corrected me.

"Can you give me a story treatment on Melissa?"

"I'd prefer she be here."

"She may never get here. People connected to Bernie seem to be at high risk. Maybe you too. Was it for your convenience or Melissa's that you two married?"

"Sorry. I really can't talk about that."

"Even if it kills you to not talk about it?"

No answer.

"Would you give me her address? I seem to have gotten it wrong."

"If you find it, would you give it to me? She's become very mysterious lately. I have no idea where she is."

It had been an illuminating conversation, but I still was not sure what had been illuminated.

I decided I wanted another talk with Melissa Franklin.

And I could only hope that it was not too late for that.

CHAPTER THIRTEEN

When I left Charles Franklin's place in Glendale I felt I had the pieces for the puzzle but wasn't seeing how to put them together, and it was driving me crazy.

Maybe that was why it took me a couple of minutes to realize I had picked up a tail car at Franklin's. My first thought was a police tail, and I was reasonably certain it hadn't followed me up that hill because night had come while I was at the Wiseman place in San Marino and you do not drive the Glendale hills at night without lights.

Next thought was that the bodies of Forta and Rodriguez had been discovered at my place and now I was, again, on the want-list. It was a logical assumption . . . they had gone to my place with a search warrant, and it was past time that someone would begin to wonder what had become of them.

I tried to lose the tail. Didn't work through two

switchback turns and a high-speed run along the Glendale Freeway. But nobody else joined in the chase, so I had to revise my reading as well as my response.

I left the freeway at Calle Verdugo and swung toward downtown Glendale with the tail intact, ducked into a small shopping center and parked in front of a liquor store. The other car eased on past and parked at the curb just beyond the entrance to the parking lot. Couldn't see the occupant but it was a late model Honda sedan with personalized plates—not an official police vehicle.

I went on into the liquor store and bought a pack of cigarettes, paused outside at a pay phone for a shot at Abe Johnson but could not connect, then sat in the Cad eyeing the Honda and trying to figure it.

Obviously someone other than cops of either force was interested in me and my movements. Someone had invaded my office, someone had invaded my home. Now someone was tailing me through the streets of Glendale. Why? Nothing computed, so I went for a direct answer.

The guy was sitting there in the Honda with the windows up and the doors locked, man of about thirty wearing a business suit and a worried face. I leaned on the roof and started it rocking, then shattered the window glass on the passenger side with the heel of my hand and opened the door. He was trying to start the car when I snatched the keys and tossed them into the rear.

"Put your wallet on the seat." I kept my tone as mild as possible under the circumstances.

The guy complied without a murmur of protest. I picked up the wallet and went back to my car to check it out. It contained fifty-two bucks, credit cards and a small detachable ID folder with a California driver's license in one window and a studio security ID in the other. The studio was *United Talents,* the name on the ID was Walter Guilder. The name meant nothing to me, but the position title did. A studio cop. Some cop. He'd taken off leaving the wallet in my possession without a murmur.

I decided to go out of my way to return the wallet. The studio was only about ten minutes away. Guilder's ID passed me through the automated gate at the employee entrance. It was nearing nine o'clock and the whole place seemed buttoned down for the night, the parking area almost empty. I took a space near the executive offices reserved for "Studio Security" and entered through a rear door. It was not a particularly large building, had two U-shaped floors with wide corridors, small offices, a front reception lobby now manned by a uniformed studio cop watching a small portable television—not closed-circuit but a rerun of "Gilligan's Island."

I surprised the guard from his backside, flustered him a bit. "Did you see Guilder come in?"

"Who, sir?"

"Walter Guilder, Security. Is he here?"

The guard switched off the TV. "Guess I don't know Mr. Guilder, sir, but I'm sure the building's empty. I mean, I thought it was."

I placed the wallet on the desk. "He left this in my car. See that he gets it back."

I left the guard impressed and flustered as he eyed the wallet and I went upstairs. I'd already checked the directory and knew where to look for Wiseman's offices. They were behind locked glass doors, had a

glitzy reception area large enough to seat a dozen
visitors in comfort, boardroom-style doors set into the
back wall.

The glass doors were no problem but it took me
minutes to get past the other ones and into a smaller
lobby. Other doors opened to my touch into a conference room, a small secretarial office and the inner
sanctum—a suite of rooms outfitted for work and re-
laxation, also physical therapy equipment and a
whirlpool bath.

I didn't exactly know what I was doing there. I'd
come on impulse—opportunistic impulse—and now
that I had it I didn't know what to do with it.

So I went into Wiseman's private office and sat on
the edge of his mahogany desk and wondered. A
movie or TV cop might rifle the desk or file cabinet
and out would pop the big clue or solution. But real
life . . . Well, what the hell, I did go through the desk
but nothing popped out at me. The man was too incredibly neat: couple of old shooting scripts, a neat
stack of legal-size ruled tablets, box of blue pencils,
a thin breast-pocket-size business diary embossed
with the Platinum Card emblem. I pocketed the diary
and kept on looking, but it was just the usual stuff.

There was no chair behind that desk, which made
me think of the wheelchair, which in turn made me
wonder about a second-floor office for a man with
nonfunctional legs. Which led me to look for the elevator. I found it behind a door in the therapy room
and took it down to a private entrance off the parking
lot and went on out that way.

A big white stretch limousine sat just outside. It
looked like the one that had brought the client to my
office at the beginning of this business, except that

this one had a different interior arrangement. Instead of a divan-seat in the rear it had a single swiveling seat with arm rests and floor mounts for a wheelchair.

I carry a "ladies' helper" in the trunk of my car—a little steel strap about eighteen inches long, like a hacksaw blade without teeth, fine little aid for those who lock their keys inside the car away from home. I went to the Cad and got it, popped the doorlock on the limo, searched the glove box. It too was incredibly neat, especially compared to my own. Vehicle Owner's Manual, registration papers in the name of *United Talents,* a rack of audiotapes—all operatic, *Aida* and *Otello* stick in the mind.

I was about to close it up when I noted the edge of a road map that apparently had become misplaced and was wedged into a small space between the top of the box and the panel. I managed to get a finger up in there and coax the map clear. It was a California road map, neatly folded to a detail of the Palm Springs area and marked with a circled number. I put the map in my pocket and shook down the rest of the car but it was clean.

It was not what I found but what found me at *United Talents* that changed that night. I'd been sprawled across the front seat while I dug for treasure in the creases. I came out backward and turned into the muzzle of a big silver revolver that found dock space at the tip of my nose. The hand that held it was as big as mine and certainly as competent, thumb on hammer in a knowledgeable fashion and discouraging rash acts.

"Is this the guy?" said a voice behind the gun.

My new pal Walt Guilder responded to that query.

He stood beside the other man and was looking at me with the purest hatred. "Yeah, bad Joe Copp. Blow the asshole away."

I delicately pushed at the barrel of the pistol with an index finger, smiled prettily and told them, "I'll tell you why I sent for you."

Nobody laughed.

At last I had a small clue.

Guilder had called me by name.

Which eliminated the possibility I'd been considering that he'd crossed my path by chance at Glendale, or at least it put a dent in it.

So maybe *now* I was going to find out why a *United Talents* security cop had been on stakeout at Charlie Franklin's, why he had followed me from there, and how he knew me on sight.

Maybe.

CHAPTER FOURTEEN

ndrew "Butch" Cassidy was head of security at *United Talents,* a bear of a man weighing some three hundred pounds with little suggestion of bodyfat in his stance. He did not speak, he barked, and that voice had been born and bred in the Bronx with little adulteration since. Maybe forty-five, fifty-five, probably somewhere in between, and I guessed accurately he'd been a New York cop.

Pedigree shows to those in the trade, and he had me pegged too—something in the walk, maybe—but he kept his big silver pistol in plain sight as he and Guilder escorted me into the security office. "Why'd you leave the force?" he barked at me as we stepped inside.

"Same reason for you, probably."

"I pensioned off. You didn't stick that long. Why not?"

Guilder didn't like the personal turn. "Watch this

guy, Butch. He's mean. Broke my window with his bare hand."

Butch Cassidy gave a disgusted look and holstered his weapon. "Didn't break your face, though. Get the man some coffee, Walter. Put some JD in it. Same for me. Then get out of here."

I sat down on a leather couch and watched the squelched junior cop play bartender and waiter while the other one went through my wallet. I got heavy black coffee laced with Jack Daniels from the one and a sour smile from the other as he tossed the wallet back to me. Guilder gave me a parting look that was like a promise, but not another word.

"You're in trouble, mister," Cassidy told me as he picked up his cup and settled behind the desk.

"Tell me about it," I said. "I've already been charged with conspiracy in several murders. What can you add to that?"

He tasted his drink. "Stupid."

"Agreed. But it gets the attention."

"Sure does. Maybe you'n me need to get together on this."

I tasted my drink, looked him over. "Okay. What're we putting together?"

"First off, I never worked for Wiseman."

"No?"

"No. You read the newspapers? *Daily Variety?*— *Hollywood Reporter?*—those kind of papers?"

"Not usually."

"Know anything about the trouble Wiseman was having with his board of directors?"

"Not the particulars, no."

"Man's a crook," he said solemnly.

"How big?"

"Big enough. Had his board worried for sure. Nickels and dimes are okay, but this guy Wiseman . . . well, they sent me out here a year ago. I report directly to Harry Klein. Know who he is?"

I admitted my ignorance.

"He's chairman of the board. Also a director of some big Wall Street outfits. The people in Manhattan have been worried about your friend Wiseman."

"Hey, I'm not sure I ever met the man."

"Then what's your interest?"

"My own neck, among other things."

"Then watch where the nose goes. Word is out that you're nosing around in other people's business. That could get you in a whole lot of trouble. Sure you never heard of Harry Klein?"

"Doesn't he sell men's suits?"

"Wising off won't help either. Klein is connected, if you get my meaning, in all the right places. He manages a great deal of money for some very important men."

I thought oh shit but said aloud, "Good for him. Myself, I'm not interested. I'd sort of like to stay out of jail and keep my license—that's my only interest. What's yours?"

"Guess I'm interested in helping you stay out of jail and out of trouble."

"Why?"

He spread his hands in a benevolent gesture. "Common background, maybe."

I thought not, but I smiled and told him, "Thanks, I appreciate it. So how can you help me?"

"Look, you're stirring up muddy waters, like I told you. That can get you nothing but trouble and it sounds to me like you got enough of that already. I've been authorized to offer you a deal. You give us Wiseman, we'll give you back your head . . . plus a nice cash bonus in the bargain."

I laughed.

"What's funny?"

"First off, you don't have my head. Even if you did I don't have Wiseman. If I did I'd give him to the cops. But I think he's dead, just like they say, and that's why I laughed. If the guy had something of yours, Cassidy, I think it went with him. So what can we put together now?"

The bear growled. "Get out of here, Copp, before I bust you for trespass."

I needed to hear it only once. I turned back at the door, though. "According to my information, the UT board of directors just recently reconfirmed Wiseman as CEO. Why would they do that if he's such a crook?"

I received a sour smile and a knowing look. "Can you imagine fifty million bucks, Copp?"

"Not really, no. My numbers don't run that high."

"Then I guess you couldn't imagine losing that much to a thief, could you."

I guessed I couldn't. But I guessed I could imagine why the losers would reconfirm someone who'd stolen it from them. What better way, really, to keep the guy around and in sight.

And if "connected," as applied to Harry Klein, still meant what it once meant, I could also imagine why the thief would want to drop out of sight for good, even to staging his own death. Especially if he'd lost the fifty million to his own numbered account somewhere.

So what did I have now?
Snakes, I had a bag of snakes.

I got back outside just in time to rescue the Cad from an assault by Guilder. The guy was apparently still smarting over his loss of face, and figured to restore some of it by retaliating tit for tat. I caught him with an iron bar poised over my windshield.

"Go ahead, break it," I told him. "Then I'm going to shove that bar someplace warm and keep it there."

He tried to laugh it off, then came to me with the bar.

I took it in the palm and kept it, hoisted him with the other hand onto the roof of the Honda. "I apologize for busting your window. I brought your wallet back."

"I got it . . ."

"So let's just call it square."

I let him down and gave him back the bar. "No reason we can't be friends then."

Actually he seemed anxious to be friends. I took the iron bar back and examined it, hefted it, placed it against my head for a fit, handed it back to him. "Were you at my office yesterday, Walt?"

The question seemed to add to his nervousness. "I don't know where your office is at, Joe."

"Lady next door described you perfectly," I lied.

"Not me, I've never been out there. I stick pretty close to—"

"Out where?"

"You said—"

"I just said my office, Walt."

"Well, I knew you're from out around Covina or Azusa, that area. I never go out there." He tried to smile. "Anything east of civic center is another country to me."

"Butch thinks you're with Wiseman."

"What?"

"He thinks you helped Wiseman set up this scam."

"Why would he think that?"

I kept on lying. "He knows about Melissa."

"How could he—?" Guilder caught himself, gave me a stage wink, tried to smirk, and, "Has to be some bonus to this work, Joe. If the lady wants to play, hey . . ."

"Don't try that with Butch, he's a bear. Bear'll eat you alive. Myself, I don't care. But the people back East want the fifty million, want it bad. I've heard of people like them hanging guys like you on a meat hook through the rectum and skinning them alive. So from one private cop to another . . ."

I now had Walter Guilder's full attention. He leaned against his car, looked me in the eye and told me in sober tones, "I don't have the fifty mil, Joe."

"Well, they're going to think so. They know about you and Melissa. They know about Charlie Franklin. And they believe that Bernie Wiseman is still alive."

"This is crazy, Joe. I bought into nothing like this. What can I do to square myself?"

I said, "I'm sort of on the same spit. Maybe we ought to put our heads together and see what we can do about it."

That made him nervous again. "I don't know, I just don't know. Did Butch tell you that?"

"Sure."

"I just don't know . . ."

"I need to talk to Melissa, Walt. Maybe I can cut a deal with these guys."

"What kind of deal?"

"Throw them some different meat."

"Oh. I see what you mean."

"So how about it?"

"How about what?"

"Set me up with Melissa."

"I don't know . . ."

"Hey, wait, it's her or us."

"I don't *want* their damned money."

"We'll have to prove it," I said. "Set me up with Melissa."

"I'll try."

"Meet me at midnight. Hollywood Bowl, lower parking lot. You'll recognize my car."

"Yeah, okay. I'll try."

"Anything beats a meat hook, Walt. Hold that thought."

Guilder looked like he'd have no trouble doing that. "Better her than us, yeah."

CHAPTER FIFTEEN

I still was interested in my official police status so I stopped at a public phone and gave Abe Johnson another try. I'd left my name on the earlier attempt, told the fellow I'd be checking back in a little while. I knew that the hour did not matter. A man in Johnson's position would be spending more time at work than at home with a case like this one. It also figured that I would get through to him this time, especially if I was hot.

I was hot, all right. First thing he said to me was, "You been home today, Joe?"

"Yeah, but I thought it best not to hang around."

"You know about Forta?"

"Yes. I'm trying to run it down, Abe, so don't game me. And forget about trying to trace the call, because I'm out of here in seconds."

He sighed and told me, "I'm not tracing it, and you're not suspected of gunning down Forta and his partner. It was the same gun used in the other shootings. But Edgar put out a pickup on you. Wants to talk to you in the worst way. Figures you know more than you've let on. Maybe are even partly responsible . . . Anyway this has to be our last conversation until you've talked to Edgar."

I said, "It's a weird case. Involves a lot of weird people. I guess you've talked to the same ones I've talked to. How does it rate on your nut-meter?"

"Pretty high."

"Have you spoken with a guy named Cassidy at UT?"

"One of my officers did."

"Give you anything?"

"Not especially. Seems to think that Wiseman is still alive. We know better."

I said, "Give it to me again, please. Just how positive is that identification?"

"As good as it can get. The forensics people are dead certain, you should pardon the expression. Wiseman had been under constant medical care since an accident in Mexico a couple years ago, confined to a wheelchair ever since. His doctors handed over the full medical file, X rays and all. It's a solid make, Joe, no matter how tantalizing other possibilities might sound."

"Then how come Edgar is still holding out for a ringer? What could he know that you don't know?"

"Beats me. He'll have to take his case to the D.A. tomorrow, so I guess we'll know soon enough."

"Have you heard anything about a missing fifty million dollars?"

"*No.* Have you?"

"Just a few minutes ago. It's got the ring of truth,

it's the first thing I've met up with in this case that could account for all the killing. Tell me, Abe, was Wiseman counterfeiting his own movies and selling them on the black market?"

"An interesting idea, but I have no evidence of anything like that. The underground film lab, sure, but so far nothing to tie it to Wiseman."

"Who owns *NuCal Designs?*"

"Two of the victims owned it—the business, not the building."

"Who owns the building?"

"An outfit back East, a bank holding-company."

"Have you checked them out?"

"We've made some inquiries."

"Take a direct look at that angle, Abe. Look especially for connections between UT and that holding company. At the highest levels. There seems to be a possibility that UT was funded with mob money."

"Okay, thanks, we'll look at that. What's this about fifty million . . . ?"

"Somebody back East maybe thinks that Wiseman was skimming on them."

"Where'd you get this?"

"From Cassidy, the security honcho. He tells me he was sent out here by the UT chairman himself, fellow named Klein, to put an eye on Wiseman. Or words to that effect. Cassidy is an ex–New York cop. He's sharp and could be mean. You might want to run a make on him, too, just for the hell of it."

"We're doing that," Johnson told me.

"Good . . . Where's Melissa Franklin?"

"Beats me," Abe said. "Where do you figure her in this?"

"Don't have that yet, but I think she could be in

some danger. She told me yesterday just before I was conked that someone wants her dead. She also told me that the man in the limousine just before it blew up was not Bernie Wiseman. And here's another. Wiseman's widow hinted at some unusual personal tie between Wiseman and the chauffeur, Albert Moore."

"Who was once married to Melissa," Johnson picked it up. "Did she mention Moore?—Melissa, I mean, when she said Wiseman wasn't in the car."

"Not that I recall. She acted kind of jangled, Abe, and I'm not *sure* that the whole thing wasn't rigged. I *think* I know who conked me, and it now appears Melissa knows, too, and that she was there with the guy—who knows why?—when I walked in on them."

"Who do you think conked you?"

"A guy named Walter Guilder, works for Cassidy . . . Oh, something else, didn't think of it until a while ago, where is Wiseman's wheelchair?"

"What d'you mean?"

"I mean, where is it now? Was it in the wreckage of the bombed limo?"

"I don't know, Joe. We'll check that out . . ."

"That could be important if—"

Abe's voice had sounded flat and sort of remote throughout our conversation. Now it leaped at me with urgency and regret. "I lied to you, Joe. Beat it quick, they've got you traced . . ."

Well, I knew what that cost Abe. If I heard it, everyone else on the line heard it too—and it figured that there were quite a few of those.

I'd left my car on the other side of a public lot a block away. Every police car in the area would have it on their hotlist and I knew that there would be police cars in the area right soon.

So I went the other way, through an alley and a shopping center and into a bowling alley two blocks farther along as cops converged on that phone booth from every direction. I could hear them tearing around the neighborhood in a search, and I knew how close it had been.

I bowled a couple of lines to wait it out inconspicuously, had a hamburger and a beer and then walked back to my car.

It was ten o'clock. I had two hours to kill until my date with Guilder at the Hollywood Bowl, just over the hill.

But all I could think of was Abe Johnson and the price he must have paid to help his wife's ex-husband avoid arrest.

It took some special kind of person to lay it all out that way.

I still couldn't put it all together yet but it was sure gnawing at me. I had a man claiming to be Albert Moore but by all appearances Bernie Wiseman, a flamboyant Hollywood figure and just possibly the most successful figure in a town where success is everything, traveling all the way out to the San Gabriel Valley in a rented limo to hire a small-time private cop for a routine nickel-and-dime job that made no sense at all on the face of it—unless he was staging his own death all along and either succeeded, or failed, spectacularly.

I had an interlude with a smashing lady once a

porno star and once married to the real Albert
Moore, now frequent companion to the ersatz
Moore—who in earlier days had made a killing
with cheapie sexploitation pictures—not making
pictures for the man but apparently content to star
in his private fantasies, accompanying him on the
San Gabriel trek but later denying it, claiming to
be in danger herself but also denying that her lover
had been killed.

I had a nonbereaved widow who might not actually
be a widow but would consider it only an inconve-
nience either way, who denounced one woman as a
whore while hip-deep in wicked pleasures herself
and accused by her husband of contracting his murder in Mexico two years earlier.

I had a couple of security cops who didn't act the
role and seemed more disturbed by missing money
than by, let's see, fifteen murders—and who, in the
final accounting, would be directly responsible for all
the killings.

Then there was the self-professed gay celibate
screenwriter who had married a porno star but neither slept nor lived with her and . . .

Gnawing, yes, all of it was gnawing at me and I
just could not get the full handle on it. Hints of
mob money and mob justice in a boardroom atmo-
sphere, treachery and thievery and sleaze of every
stripe, murder and mayhem and cop-killing, and it
could be all over a couple of lousy bucks—*okay,*
fifty million is not a couple and bucks are not of
themselves lousy. But great numbers of them are
usually accompanied by anger and cynicism and
mindless violence.

Enough to turn your stomach. Which was the state of my gut. Turned. Turning.

I bowled a 210 and a 218 minutes after I probably wrecked the fine police career of my second wife's black husband. The highest two games of my life, at the lowest of its moments.

CHAPTER SIXTEEN

It seemed a party was in progress. The circular drive was stuffed with expensive cars and the whole place was ablaze with lights. I didn't want to be a distraction so I kicked the door open and went in unannounced, startling the attractive maid who looked even more attractive this time. She wore a fluffy black lace outfit with too-high heels. Like those Playboy bunnies, she had to smile in her ridiculous outfit. Right now, though, I didn't have time for more than passing compassion as I told her to take off, which she did with pleasure toward the rear of the house.

I could hear party sounds from that direction and went the other way, up the stairs and through six bedrooms, uncovered a pair of lesbian lovers so involved they didn't notice me. Nothing else up there.

I met Justine Wiseman on the stairway as I was going back down. She was customed for an S-M film of her own—garter belt, black fishnet stockings, high-heeled kneeboots, black silver-studded leather bra with nipple cutouts, brandishing a riding crop. She swung at me with the crop. I took it on the arm and pinned her to the railing. "Try it again and I'll put that thing where it'll do you the most good." I meant every word of that.

"What are you doing here, where's your search warrant? I'll have your job—"

"Someone beat you to it," I told her, and went on down the stairs and toward the sounds of party.

Justine ran along behind me, cussing and threatening me with every manner of vile punishment. She no doubt meant every word too. I shook down a couple of rooms along the way, again found nothing except a man's electric shaver in a hallway bathroom, and arrived at the gym with Justine now half-hanging on my back.

There were a couple dozen people in there—mostly female—and all dressed for Sodom-and-Gomorrah motif. The guests were having a shriekingly good time at the expense of a stud being led about on hands and knees with a dog collar around his neck and no clothing on his body.

I felt a little sick as I looked at that guy, partly because I recognized him, partly because it was just a scene to be made sick by. The guy was trying to mount the women but was being jerked away and "punished" at the crucial moment, much to the delight of the assembled.

Another scenario was being acted out on top of the massage table, where two nude young women glistening with oil were snaking around each other to a disco beat while a naked stud tried to insert himself between them.

I guess if any of the guests noticed Justine and me, we were just another part of the bizarre festivities. I did not see anyone else in there I knew or recognized until the Viking warrior lady made her entrance via the bathroom, accompanied by the maid. She made a lunge for me. I handed her Justine instead and invaded the doggy circle, intent on snaring the leash and leading that doggy away to my own idea of party—

Something exploded against the small of my back, I found myself on my knees on the mat. Another explosion to the rib cage put me on my back. I caught a bare foot in the hand just before it would have found its way to my face.

The Viking warrior was pretty good with her feet, good enough with everything else, I figured, to be disqualified for weaker-sex considerations, so I tossed that foot and its attachments as far as I could, and two hundred pounds, give or take, of naked Viking took a header into the squealing crowd.

She bounced right back, though, began circling me like a Sumo wrestler. I thought, who needed this, but I was stuck with it, and suddenly Viking and Copp were the star act. I set her down one more time with a simple one-two to the chin, down onto her iron ass, where she stayed in dulled surprise. I guess it surprised the guests, too, because it became very quiet as realization dawned that the party was over.

I turned back to the doggy but he was gone. I looked for him throughout the house and grounds and all the cars, twice, but he was definitely gone.

Which was very disappointing to me.

Because that doggy, I was pretty sure, was the chauffeur, Albert Moore.

It just didn't figure that he would show himself at a party only days after supposedly being blown to bits by a car-bomb.

Justine stonewalled it, of course, insisting that I'd not seen what I knew I had seen. The guy on the leash was definitely the same one who had stepped into my office wearing a chauffeur's uniform, the same one who had taken my delivery of exposed film at the corner of Melrose and La Brea—the same whose supposed remains had been found and forensically identified as those of Albert Moore.

There had been a wild exodus from that San Marino mansion following my little bout with the Viking, even a couple of fender-crunchers in the excitement, the sort of panic often displayed at the scene of a police raid. It figured that many of the guests led double-lives and had too much to lose by public disclosure of their presence at a sex party with perverse overtones—I understate, of course. My first impression had been accurate: only two men had been present, and both had been acting out group fantasies of male degradation. Both also had disappeared while I was diverted by the attack of the warrior woman.

I stood outside and jotted down license tags during that panicky exodus, then went back inside to confront Justine again. She was appropriately furious with me, alternately cussing and crying, but the Viking was strangely subdued. She had put on a terry-

cloth robe and was sitting on the massage table
glumly watching me as I tried to settle Justine down.
I kept her in the corner of an eye, though. My back
still hurt from her attack and it pained to take a deep
breath.

Justine finally flounced into her bedroom and
locked the door. Okay, I figured I wasn't going to get
anything more there anyway, but the VW came back
to life as I was leaving.

"You could be an interesting man," she told me in,
I swear, seductive tones.

I said smartly, "Thanks, so could you."

"No, I'm serious."

"More interesting than the two you had in here a
while ago?"

"I didn't notice them."

Sure she didn't.

"You noticed me, why not them? Looked to me like
the other girls were having a great time with them."

She made a face. "You get past that after a while,
doesn't turn me on anymore."

I said, "Does Albert come often?"

She said, "Albert who?"

"Albert Doggy."

"Oh," she said, "that's not an Albert, that's an Algernon."

"What's an Algernon?"

"An Algernon," she explained to her stupid pupil,
"is just the opposite of a Beowulf."

"And what," I asked, playing the game, "is a Beowulf?"

"*You* are a Beowulf. Will you teach me to box?"

"Not tonight, Josephine. Unless you'd like to teach
me about Albert."

"Algernon."

"Okay, that'll do for starters—"

But she had dropped the robe, clearly looking for another go-round.

She crouched and pivoted on her left foot, came whirling out of the crouch with a high kick toward the head. I sidestepped it, considered and discarded the notion of a more physical defense, and got the hell out of there before I became another damned doggy in the window.

CHAPTER SEVENTEEN

*T*he Hollywood Bowl is nestled into the hills off Cahuenga Boulevard. Before they built the freeways, Cahuenga was the major route through the Hollywood hills and into the San Fernando Valley, following a natural canyon just west of Griffith Park. You can take Cahuenga all the way to Studio City, where it becomes Ventura Boulevard, the old Highway 101 and still the main street for many of the valley communities such as Sherman Oaks, Encino, Tarzana and Woodland Hills.

Most of the through traffic these days is along the freeway routes. Cahuenga at midnight can be virtually deserted, especially in the Bowl area when nothing is happening at the amphitheatre. Nothing was happening that night. It's a parklike setting with lots of grass and picnic tables. For summer concerts many people like to come early with a picnic basket and make an evening of it. But it was very quiet around there when I rolled in for my midnight rendezvous with Guilder and, one hoped, Melissa Franklin. There's a parking lot below the Bowl in the picnic and snack bar area—now deserted and not too well lit in the vapory mists of the night. I had figured it to be that way when I set up the meet, and I had come in along the back side via Cahuenga from Universal City, assuming that my car was still hot and hoping to avoid contact with the law-enforcement community.

I was ten minutes early, the way I like it for this sort of thing. I put the Cad at the top of the lot, where the mists were heaviest, nose-out and free to travel with minimum restriction, then got into my gun harness and found comfort in the darkness about fifty feet away.

Had the whole place to myself for fifteen minutes. Nothing moved or showed until midnight plus five, when a police car cruised through the turnaround and went on back without stopping. Ten minutes later I was wondering if I'd come for nothing. The evening chill was settling into me and I was thinking about taking off when the Jaguar pulled in down below. It stopped just inside and sat there for a few moments, then pulled on around in a jerky, hesitant manner and stopped again on the far side.

I went to the Cad and flashed the headlights, had to do it twice before the Jaguar started moving and headed toward me. I retreated again and did not expose myself until I could see the whites of the lady's eyes. Fifteen people were dead and I had no desire to join the tally. Where was Guilder?

She pulled in beside the Cad, alone in the car and clearly nervous. I came down and rapped on the passenger side. Melissa unlocked the door and I slid in beside her, door open and one foot outside, as before. Even scared she was delicious-looking.

"Keep your hands on the wheel," I told her. "I'm going to pat you down."

"You're going to *what?*"

But I was already doing it. She was wearing a suede jacket with jeans and T-shirt, nowhere much to conceal a weapon but I'd have been a fool to take chances. As I poked around under her and beneath the seat we said nothing and she was just sitting there woodenly. Pretty much the same as before when we sat together in her car.

"Okay, where's Guilder?"

Those large eyes didn't blink. "Where is he supposed to be?"

"I thought he'd want to come along and play cop like he did last time."

She looked away. "Sorry, he panicked."

"What was he looking for in my office?"

"Answers."

"To what?"

"To this crazy business . . . I think somebody tried to kill me."

"You were supposed to have been in the limo when it blew?"

"I think so, yes. I was supposed to meet Mr. Wiseman at eight o'clock. I was a few minutes late. I got into the car and . . . and it wasn't the right car. Not the same car, I mean. And the man looked like Mr. Wiseman but it wasn't him."

"Wrong car, wrong man. Wrong chauffeur, too?"

"No . . . that's the odd part. I'm sure it was Albert. We were married for three years, I couldn't have mistaken—that was Albert."

"Definitely not Wiseman?"

"No. I mean yes. Anyway, I don't really know him all that well. I *knew,* though, that something was strange there. It sent chills down my back. I don't fight those feelings, I just react. Good thing I did, huh. I wasn't half a block away when . . ." She shivered. "I could feel the heat in my own car."

"And you kept right on running."

"I sure did. I was already starting to wonder about all this."

"All this what?"

"I mean, even before I came back. It just wasn't making sense anymore."

My data pool was getting flooded. I said, "Back from where?"

"What?"

"You said, before you came back. Back from where?"

"From Mexico. They sent me down there nearly a year ago. Made sense at the time, but now—well it all sounds kind of crazy. Then they called and told me about you and—"

"What about me?"

"That, you know, you were getting the films back."

"What films?"

"The old movies? And everything was going to be just fine and we could go ahead now. So—"

"Wait. Let me get this . . . you've been in Mexico for the past year?"

"Almost, yes, because, well they *said* because—"

"And all the time you've been married to Franklin?"

"Well, yes, see, that's . . . it sounds crazy, I know, but that was part of the package, the image thing. But that was all over, see, that part was over and they sent for me. We were meeting at eight o'clock and . . . but the damned car blew up in my face. I was scared to death, I'm still scared to death, and I was even afraid to go to the police because it all sounds so hokey. So I called Walter Guilder. We were friends a long time ago and I knew that he was in Mr. Wiseman's security force. I really had no one else to turn to. Walter decided we needed to find out exactly what you were doing for Mr. Wiseman, and that's why we went to your office yesterday."

She'd become a wind-up talking doll and was showing no signs of winding-down. Which was okay, she was venting and that was good, talking herself back to sanity, and I was willing to let her do it—I was eager for her to do it—but we had not yet reached the rational level and I was just trying to guide her toward it.

"You see, they'd told me all about you, your background with the regular police and all, that you were this straight-arrow guy and could be depended on for discretion, that you were so thorough and had this great reputation and all, and . . ."

I'd lost track of what she was saying because my attention was distracted by movements down below. The fog was really settling in heavy and even the light standards were hardly more than faint shrouded beacons in the gloom, so the visibility had fallen rapidly. The occasional cars moving along Cahuenga were just dim globs of light in an ethereal background. So I didn't know exactly what I was seeing down there in the turnaround, but it seemed like a car or cars moving without lights through the fog.

I closed my door to extinguish the dome light and

put a hand on Melissa's mouth to shush her as I asked, "Is Guilder down there?"

She said, "He thought we should come in separate cars, but he should be here by now. I think he's very nervous about all this."

"How good a friend is Guilder?"

"We met in an acting class. That's all. We just knew each other. Never dated or anything like that. Ran into each other at the studio last year and he told me he'd given up acting and liked his new work very much. So naturally I thought of him when—"

"Frying pan to the fire maybe, kid. Tell me something, what's the first thing to come to your mind when you hear the phrase fifty million bucks?"

I could not see her face too clearly now but those eyes were only inches from mine and I thought I could see something happening in there as she said, "What do you mean?"

"Means nothing to you?"

"Well sure, it means *some*thing to me. But what do *you* mean?"

"Something worth dying for, maybe. Or killing for."

"I don't understand."

Neither did I, not exactly.

I asked her pointblank, "Are you a whore?"

Eyes flashed at me across the darkness but it took a couple of beats for her to reply. "That's a hell of a thing to say."

"Didn't say it. Someone else did. I'm asking. Are you?"

"Depends on the definition, I guess," her voice suddenly weary. "I've never stood on a streetcorner, if that's what you mean."

"Were you Wiseman's woman?"

"No."

"You never lived with him, slept with him, rubbed his back, drove around town at his feet in the limo and kept him comforted?"

"Never did," she said quietly.

"You didn't come to my office with him earlier this week hiding behind sunglasses?"

"No, I did not."

"When did you get back from Mexico?"

"Tuesday afternoon, to meet him at eight in Hollywood."

"You didn't come to my office on Monday?"

"I told you, no. I was in Mexico Monday."

"Can you prove that? Airline ticket or—?"

"I drove up."

"In this car?"

"Yes. I left Monday morning, spent the night near Tijuana, came on in the next day."

"Starting where?"

"Baja. Mr. Wiseman has a place on the ocean near San Quintin. It's about a four-hundred-mile drive to Tijuana."

"You were staying at Wiseman's place?"

"Yes."

"Did he give you the car?"

"Yes. It was a wedding gift."

"When you married Franklin."

"Yes."

"What sort of dues did you pay to get it?"

"In this business, the usual. But the personalized tags were Mr. Wiseman's idea too. He wanted me to think of the whole year that way."

"The year in Mexico."

"Yes."

"How did your new husband want you to think of that year?"

Silence.

I tried another. "Why was Guilder staking out your husband's house earlier today?"

"Was he?"

My talking doll had run down and was becoming very guarded again. Never mind. This girl was the master key. Either she was giving it to me straight or she was a damned fine actress. To believe her, I first had to believe that she was indeed Melissa Franklin. Then I had to believe that someone was playing a most tricky game with stand-ins and stuntmen, false fronts and special effects—a real Hollywood production. But why not? These were Hollywood people, after all. First, though, I had to convince myself that this was the real Melissa Franklin, be patient until she came up with—

What came up was gunfire, a volley of three quick shots followed by two from a different gun, coming from somewhere down in the gloom of the turn-around.

I shoved Melissa onto the floorboards and took off running with gun in hand toward the sounds. But I got there a couple of shots too late. Both of them had gone into Walter Guilder's head, and there was nobody else around but me.

The death count had risen to sixteen, and the answer to it all nearly ran me down as she powered the dues-paid Jaguar through the latest killing ground and onto Cahuenga boulevard.

Even her headlights were instantly swallowed by the fog. The living doll was running again.

CHAPTER EIGHTEEN

I'd heard tires screeching on pavement down there while I was closing on that scene, and I found shattered auto glass thirty feet from Guilder's Honda. He was slumped over his steering wheel with two gunshot wounds in the face. A pistol lay on the seat beside him. Not too difficult to reconstruct the action. Evidently he'd fired first, broadside through the open window that I'd broken earlier, and the return fire had come back at him via the same route because the windshield and other areas looked good as new. Either someone was a hell of a marksman or got very lucky from thirty feet away.

I was kneeling on the asphalt and looking at the broken window glass when Melissa had come out of the fog in her Jaguar. I didn't think she was trying to run me down. I doubt she even saw me. She was just trying to get the hell away from there. As I dove for the grass to get out of her way I was deciding that she had the best idea of the moment. Those shots must have been heard all the way down at Hollywood and Vine. Police response could be quick.

I ran back to the Cad and beat it out of there too, running without lights until I was moving clear and free down the hill. Cahuenga is split at that point, southbound lanes west of the freeway and northbound on the other side. I could hear the police sirens up the north leg before I traversed the split, it was that close. I went on down Cahuenga and swung west on Sunset. The visibility was much better down there and the traffic light. I kept hoping to spot the Jaguar but of course I didn't.

I also didn't know where I was going or should go. I just knew it was not smart to be cruising Hollywood at that time of night in a hot car. I had already beat down an urge to duck over to my friend Nancy's for another go at sanctuary. She lives only five minutes from the Bowl and I was sure she'd let me in again. But that would buy me nothing but a bit of rest, and I didn't feel like resting. I still needed answers, not comforting.

Why the gunfight at the Hollywood Bowl? What had that bought anyone? To listen to Melissa tell it, Guilder had just been trying to help a friend in need—and I felt like maybe it was true. The guy had liked to talk tough but he was a lightweight mixing it up with the heavies, and I just couldn't see him as a bad guy in this piece. An actor—okay—I could see it, a make-believe tough guy, and he'd come to grief fast in the real world. Melissa said that he'd panicked at my office when he conked me; maybe he'd panicked again and started shooting when a couple of toots of a horn would have served the moment better.

If he'd been down there acting as a lookout, and if Melissa had mentioned her midnight meeting to the wrong person . . . it could have gone down that way. Or maybe Guilder himself had let it drop to someone—maybe someone like Butch Cassidy.

I kept moving out Sunset and found myself on the Strip before I knew it. Beverly Hills was just around the corner and then Bel Air . . . Maybe I'd been on that heading subconsciously all the way. I pulled over at the Comedy Club to consult Abe Johnson's extract of the case, found Wiseman's Bel Air address and located it on my map.

Beverly Hills is its own city, you know. Bel Air is not. It is a section of Los Angeles and probably the most expensive turf inch-for-inch in the city, sits just west of Beverly Hills and north of UCLA, east of the San Diego Freeway and nestled into the canyons of the Santa Monica Mountains. It has gated entrances off Sunset, and the terrain behind those gates creates a natural maze from which the most determined tourists often emerged dazed and shaken after wandering through it for hours. I don't recommend that you venture in there, especially at night, without a finely detailed road map of the neighborhood.

I found the Wiseman palace off Bellagio Drive, one of the main roads, for which I was very grateful, and I proceeded to play second-story man. Had to scale a wall and move through a half acre of natural booby traps in the stygian darkness, then had to go around an electronic security system and climb a balcony to an upstairs window to get inside the house.

This place made Justine's San Marino digs look like poor relatives. I had to wonder what a fifty-year-old paraplegic needed with a place like this.

According to the record Wiseman had never been a social lion, rarely entertained at home and had been antisocial since his accident.

Well, I had the place to myself. Johnson's notes indicated that the household staff had been dismissed even before Wiseman's death and that a lone housekeeper lived in a guest house at the rear. All the furniture was covered, and the place felt like a mausoleum. I found the kitchen, which could have prepared state banquets. Everything draped, disconnected, deactivated.

I wandered about in the dark, using a pencil-flash now and then, found a library and a study and a game room and a ballroom.

What was more important was what I did not find there. During my years as a cop I have been inside many homes of deceased people. A home can reveal a person—even a dead one—at least some of the personality and character values. It was why I was here.

I found no magazines in Wiseman's house, dusty-layered books that looked never to have been taken down off the shelves—strange for an ex–whiz kid—no newspapers, no photographs, no bills paid or unpaid, no food, no booze, no clothing, no cosmetics, no trace whatever of the man or how he might have lived there.

Of course the man was dead—but only very recently. Why should every trace have been wiped away so quickly?

I'd never seen the likes of it, and I wasn't buying it.

I went to the guest cottage and woke up the housekeeper—a vigorous-looking woman of indeterminate middle years who slept in an old-fashioned flannel nightgown and nightcap and had further bundled herself in a heavy chiffon robe to answer the door.

I showed her my ID and apologized for the intrusion, told her I urgently needed to talk with her. She spoke with a heavy European accent—maybe German or Dutch—and seemed flustered by my visit. She insisted on making coffee, which sounded fine to me, so we went into her kitchen and I made myself comfortable in a little breakfast nook at the window. She didn't ask how I'd gotten onto the grounds and I was hoping she wouldn't; it was obvious she thought I was a public cop. I've found that people from Europe tend to accept most anything from a cop; most of those countries don't have a bill of rights, or at least don't honor them. Her name was Edda.

"What can I help you, sir?" she asked once the coffee was on and cooking.

I told her, "I'm a bit puzzled, Edda. There's no sign of living in there. It wasn't closed up like that just since Mr. Wiseman died, was it?"

"Oh no, sir." Her hands were clasped across an ample belly. "Is the way it was."

"It has always been closed up this way?"

"Yes, sir, as same as Mr. Wiseman first come." She pronounced it *Viseman.*

"He bought the house this way, completely furnished, the way it is now?"

"Same as now, ya."

"Everything all covered up and all that?"

"Ya."

"Never wanted the covers taken off?"

"*Ya,* same as now."

"How did he live in that, Edda?"

"No no, live not in that, live in this." She opened her hands to indicate the guest cottage.

"Show me, please."

She took the coffee off the burner and led me to a large room at the rear of the cottage. It was very homey, soft and clean and simple—an all-purpose room containing a double bed, a small desk, a couch and a couple of overstuffed chairs, table by the window but no chairs at it, hardwood floor with plenty of open space and no rugs to interfere with the movement of a wheelchair.

And a wheelchair, yes, stood beside French doors at the back wall.

I said to the housekeeper, "He left his wheelchair."

"Oh *ya*—yes, sir—this chair is the home chair, not the car chair."

"He used a different chair for traveling about?"

"Oh *ya*, this chair will not . . ." She made a squeezing sign with her hands.

"Doesn't fold up."

She smiled. *"Ya.* This chair better comfort for home."

There was no television in the room but it had an elaborate audio system, compact disc player, the works. I found a whole library of Verdi's compositions, remembered the tapes I'd found in the glove box of the UT limo.

"He liked opera," I commented.

"Very much the opera. Verdi."

So the home reveals the man. I found a lot of stuff back there that told me something of Bernard Wiseman—a man of obvious sensitivity and culture, refined tastes, great intellectual capacity. Sounded like the man described to me by the screenwriter, nothing at all like the other reputation.

I said to the housekeeper, "This is where he lived, then."

"Oh *ya*," she replied proudly. "This is where he is comfortable, this is home."

"How long did you know him, Edda?"

She smiled and told me, "Not so long, but very well. Wonderful man. So young to die."

"Did you know Albert Moore?"

"Oh *ya*."

"Melissa Franklin?"

Her face tightened and she tried to cover it but not in time. *"Ya."*

"What's wrong, Edda? You don't have to hide anything from me. What's wrong with Melissa?"

She would give me nothing more than a pained smile on that subject, so I let it go. She offered to serve the coffee back there, which suited me fine. I kept on poking around while she was getting it, found nothing more of specific interest until I opened a book that was lying on the bedside table. Inserted into it like a bookmark was a polaroid snapshot. It depicted Wiseman in sunglasses similar to those worn at our meeting, seated in a compact wheelchair somewhere outside. A white limo was in the background, and a man in a chauffeur's uniform was kneeling beside the wheelchair.

I showed the snapshot to Edda when she returned with the coffee. "Do you know when that was taken?"

"Yes, sir, I take this last month."

"You took it? Who's the man in the uniform?"

"This in uniform is Albert."

"Albert Moore?"

"Ya."

"How well did you know Albert?"

"He too here lives. Over garage."

I had myself a double bingo. But at the moment I did not know exactly what to make of it.

I just knew that the chauffeur in that snapshot was not the Albert Moore I knew, or thought I knew. I had never seen that fellow before.

CHAPTER NINETEEN

I connected with a *Times* editor, fellow I'd known since my LAPD days, and he let me into their morgue to search out Wiseman, though he assured me he had already done that and could gist it for me in two minutes. I'd already been gisted; I wanted a close look for myself. The editor was very interested in the Wiseman affair, of course, and he also knew that I was hot. I promised him a lock on the story if I ever put it together for myself. He set up the equipment for me and then left me to my own devices.

I had used the equipment before, of course. The computer age . . . used to be you could spend days going through back issues and still miss the item you were looking for. Now you just punch up the program on a computer terminal, sit back and let the magic genie search through years of news quicker than you can light a cigarette. It's all cross-indexed by sub-

jects, dates, personalities, events—and you can call
up every story in the file on a given person and even
get hard copies if you want them.

There was not that much of a file on Bernard Wiseman, though the file was twenty years deep. He had
been charged once years ago with contributing to the
delinquency of a minor, charges later dropped. In
more recent years he had been honored by the Producer's Guild and attacked by the Writer's Guild,
there was a mention of his separation from Justine,
coverage of his accident in Mexico, some stuff from
the financial pages regarding UT's soaring success,
gossip-column chaff about the problems with his
board of directors, other odds and sods regarding new
projects.

Then, beginning about six months before the
bombing, there was a story at least every week in
which he was mentioned as appearing at various social functions around town, always accompanied by
Melissa Franklin, who was usually referred to as a
"rising star" or words to that effect—once as "UT's
rising new star." No mention of any of her pictures,
though. There was a flurry of stories spanning the
last several weeks—almost daily—again dealing
with the infighting at UT. The newest stuff was not
yet in the computer.

I called up the photo file and found three pictures
of interest, two of them showing Wiseman in a tux-
edo and a stunning blond wearing little more than
sunglasses, the third showing Wiseman being
wheeled out of his limo by his chauffeur at some
benefit. The blond was identified as Melissa Franklin—but who would know for sure? No identification
of the chauffeur, but it was the same man as in the

Polaroid. Not a lot of help there, but at least it deepened my suspicion that I was up against a masterly production of deception and illusion.

I needed more information from Melissa, and I wanted another crack at her husband. I also would have loved to get Justine Wiseman into a cold shower and hold her there until she turned blue enough to talk like ordinary people. And I wanted the doggy boy and maybe a crack at some of Justine's party guests.

The odds, though, were that I would be behind bars before I could get to any of those people. I had been a cop long enough to realize I was on the downward leg of my trajectory through this case—that I was running out of time, out of options.

Two magnificent police machines were chewing through the interconnections a lot faster than I could hope to. They would get to the end before I would, and I had the sinking feeling that I had been staked out as raw meat from the beginning of this thing. It was more than a feeling. Edgar had supposedly been tipped by an informant that I'd been paid big money to help Wiseman stage his death. I knew how that played in the police mind. Didn't require a lot of stretch for them to infer a whole bunch of other crimes, especially if the tip-line was still busy. Those guys weren't chasing me all over town just so they could prove me innocent. They were on my tail because the politicians on *their* tails wanted a quick wrap-up to this case and didn't much care who got burned in the process.

So I was seeing my one hope as a power play straight up the middle—forgetting finesse and fancy footwork, forgetting scenarios and weirdos and mysterious manipulations. I suspected by now that much

of that was disinformation anyway, confusion factor.
I had to take that shot up the middle.

So I asked my friend the editor to run a make for
me on Andrew "Butch" Cassidy. I mentioned the
New York connection and his position at UT, then sat
in the corner with bitter newsroom coffee and
watched my life tick away while the computer terminal flashed its magic coast-to-coast in a chase after
the facts of the matter. I said it already, it's a genie,
and it even provided me with Cassidy's Los Angeles
address and phone number.

I was out of there at four o'clock and creeping at low
silhouette through the quiet streets, up onto the
Santa Monica Freeway and fast west through the fog,
off at La Brea and northward at creep speed again
toward Farmer's Market and the CBS studios, across
Beverly and into a fashionable apartment complex.

This time it was my piece docking at his nose, and
he came up as quietly as I had. He was not sleeping
alone. She was young and out of it, sleeping facedown
and one arm dangling over the side. He grabbed his
clothes from a chair and we went quietly to the living
room, where he put them on without protest by word
or gesture. We took the elevator to the garage, got into
his car and set off for UT. So far I'd done all the
talking. We were halfway across town before he
asked me what was up.

I told him, "Life, maybe, yours and mine. I guess
it's up to you."

"What is?"

"How much longer either of us have. Looks like

your New York pals have sewn me into this thing too tight to unravel. So I'm binding you in there with me. What happens to me happens to you."

"You're nuts," he said. "Who are you? The men in New York have never heard your name."

"Then you've got nothing to worry about. Nothing happens to me and you too."

"You better tell me what's on your mind. If I'm bound to you, Copp, at least I should know who your enemies are supposed to be."

I told him, "You're my enemy, Butch."

"Bullshit. I don't—"

"You and every other kinky cop that ever dirtied a badge. I got no respect. You're filth, so don't try shining it on to me."

He didn't even try to bluster it out. "Who the hell are you to say? I didn't see no honors in your file, Mr. Boy Scout."

"Didn't work for honors, or merit badges. Obviously you didn't either. Pensioned, my ass. You were lucky to just stay on the streets. How long you been on Chairman Klein's payroll?"

"Up yours," he said. "I don't owe you anything. Let's do what you gotta do and get it over with. Exactly what d'you want?"

"Exactly I want my head out of this noose not of my making. I'm going to make you talk sense to me, Butch. One way or the other."

"With or without your gun, scout?"

"Whatever it takes. I'll shoot your knees off, I don't care, whatever language you understand best."

"Or up the nose, like you did to Walter?"

I said, "You heard, eh?"

"ID'd the body. The kid was raw. You didn't need that."

"I also didn't do that, but I was in the neighborhood when it went down. Figured you did it . . ."

"Why would *I* do it? He was my man—"

"You'd do it to your own mother. Especially with fifty mil in the kitty. Assuming there really is a fifty mil. Is there?"

"There was," he said

"I'll want you to tell me about that."

"Already did. Now you tell me about it."

"I'm the one with the gun this time. I could start with your balls if you like your knees better."

He actually smiled at that. "Neither are much good to me anymore. Notice that kid back there? Now it takes me all night to do what I used to do all night long. It's embarrassing, especially with these kids. I don't think they even know what sex is, most of 'em. Tight little pussies and empty little heads, that's all I ever get, and they don't even know what they're missing."

"They know why they're doing it," I told him. They like the color of your money."

He said, "Maybe that's the problem. Go ahead. Take the balls. I don't need 'em. At least with knees I can still peek through keyholes."

"Too late," I said. "No more keyholes."

He laughed. "Guess that dates me too. How old are you, Copp?"

"Just barely downside of forty."

"Past forty, you better start calling your shots."

"Already started it," I said. "Saved one tonight, in fact. Ever been to one of Justine's parties?"

"Justine Wiseman? Never met the lady. They were separated when I came out here."

"Did you know Wiseman before his accident?"

"The back injury? That happened about a year before I came out."

"Why'd they send you, Butch?"

"Told you. Their man was cheating 'em."

"Why didn't they send an auditor?"

He laughed. "With those guys, I am an auditor."

I didn't laugh. "Thought they called it enforcer."

"That too."

"Legbreaker."

"On occasion."

"Even wearing a badge."

"Hey, hold the holy water. Know how many cops I've buried? Never a kinky one, though. Only heroes get buried. Smart guys bury them."

"And you're one of the smartest."

"That's right."

"Did you come here to bury Wiseman?"

"Hell, no. And he's no hero. Wiseman will end up burying you."

"Think he could talk his way out of this mess?"

"Sure he could. Don't believe their movies. These guys don't have codes of honor. They have bottom-line profit motive. Turn profits for them, they love you. Even if you cheat them they love you because they respect you, and they know you can do it to others for them. He could make it up, sure. Tell Wiseman to sweeten the pot, add ten mil and give it all back. They'll even let 'im keep his job."

"Sure, suspended from a meat hook."

He laughed. "You watch too many movies. They

don't do that stuff anymore. This new generation don't even know how."

"But your generation does."

He turned a smile to me. "My generation invented it."

He was Butch Cassidy now, and he didn't need a Sundance Kid. He'd been fired, so the record said, from NYPD fifteen years ago after a long career as a mob enforcer with a badge, and he'd been suspected but never charged in a whole litany of crimes since that time. On the streets of New York they didn't call him Butch Cassidy. They called him Butcher Cassidy. Maybe he'd killed a cord of people in Los Angeles, too? Somehow I didn't think so. And I was even hoping that I wouldn't have to get too rough with him. Butcher or not, I sort of respected the way he carried himself. We had a pretty good understanding of each other by the time we reached the studio.

Besides, I had neither the time, the options nor the brains to set myself up as judge and jury. I was still a cop, trying to do a job. If that meant kissing the guy, then I'd kiss him.

If it meant killing him, I'd do that too.

CHAPTER TWENTY

We sat across the desk from each other. I placed my big pistol midway between us. "Go for it any time you'd like," I told him.

"Who needs it? I told you before, we need to get our heads together on this. So what's the beef? Let's just do it."

"Tell me again why they sent you West."

"It reads the same every time. Their boy was cheating on them. They sent me out to watch his fingers."

"Did he know they suspected?"

"Course he knew."

"They'd called him on it?"

"Sure. He'd been cheating small all along. Hey, everybody expects it. Expense accounts, petty cash, kickbacks, that's considered part of the salary if you do it cool. But this guy really lost it big, especially after the injury in Mexico. They figured he went a little nuts, brooding about that maybe. Went for a grand slam and a quick out."

"How was he doing it?"

"Right off the top."

"Top of what?"

"Top of the gross. Three sets of books. One set for the stockholders, one for the men, one for himself.

"So how'd they know for sure?"

"I found his books."

"When?"

"Just last week."

"So you sent them right off to New York."

"Took 'em myself.

"Know how this would sound in court?"

"I'd deny the hell out of it in court. You know that."

"Tell it to my pal Edgar," I suggested. "He's brilliant at building cases from bits and pieces. He's trying to wrap one around my throat right now with less to build on. Edgar would say that you came back from New York with a contract in your pocket. He'd say that you shook the fifty mil or whatever out of Bernie and then torched him along with his whole operation."

"Wouldn't sound too brilliant to me," Cassidy said. "I wouldn't do it that way."

"No?"

"No. I'd just take your friend for a drive to Las Vegas. I'd get there, he wouldn't. And I'd dare Mr. Brilliant to find the right spot to start digging up two hundred miles of desert."

I knew he was right. It had been done that way many times. I said, "So you think the bombs were for stage effect."

"Sure they were."

"And the shootings."

"I'm still wondering about those. But Wiseman's behind them, you can make book on that."

"You've been watching him for a year. See anything to suggest he might be setting up something like this?"

"No. But he wouldn't want me to see that, would he."

"He knew you were watching him?"

"Had to know. Last few months, anyway."

"You wanted him to know."

"Sure. War of nerves. Kept thinking the guy would crack and come back home on his knees."

"So now you figure he cracked the other way."

Cassidy shifted uncomfortably. "Looks that way, or else he was suckering me all the way. No . . . I think he cracked when his books came up missing. I was in New York three days waiting for the decision. Got back Monday night. It blew to hell Tuesday."

"Do you know Melissa Franklin?"

"Know of her. Pretty hot stuff."

"You've been here a year. Melissa tells me she's been in Mexico a year."

"No way. She's been humping your friend all this past year, and he has not gone near Mexico."

"You said you were in New York three days waiting for a decision. What decision was that?"

"I was told to confront Wiseman on the books and give 'im a chance to come clean. To come home, you know."

"And if he didn't?"

The old legbreaker smiled. "Then I could use my own discretion."

"Squeeze it out of him."

"Like that."

"You didn't try that, though."

"Didn't get the chance."

"Maybe you did, at least maybe Edgar would think you did. You recovered the fifty mil and decided to keep it for yourself. But you had to cover your tracks. So you blew up all the tracks and now you're just sitting and waiting the air to clear."

"Sure. And retire to Argentina."

"Could be."

"Sure it could. But it didn't turn that way."

"But aren't you a little worried that the men in New York might wonder if it did?"

"It occurred to me. Why do you think I'm in such a sweat, birdbrain? Maybe I have to find the guy if only to square myself. Think I'd be hanging around for any other reason? If I had the fifty I'd have already found somewhere else to count it."

"What's with Guilder?"

"Raw kid, but he tried hard."

"You had him tailing Wiseman?"

He nodded.

"Ever wonder if Guilder was square with you?"

"No reason to wonder. He loved to play cops and robbers. Not too quick between the ears but . . . I trusted him."

"He ever mention Melissa Franklin to you?"

"Don't think so, except maybe in routine reports. Why?"

"They've known each other for years. He ran into her just before she went to Mexico. So the memory was fresh. If he was shadowing Wiseman, and if she really was in Mexico all that time, don't you think he would've spotted a stand-in?"

"I don't get it. Why would she have a stand-in? The girl was not in Mexico, Copp. She was right here in L.A. and on Wiseman's arm most every time he went out."

"Melissa says she was in Mexico. As I get it, something to do with a plan to launder her past and then bring her back a bright new discovery. No more porno. She was called home this last weekend, got here Tuesday just in time for the fireworks. She thinks she was meant to join the fireworks. And she says that Bernie Wiseman was not in that limo."

"I want to talk with that lady," Cassidy said.

I told him, "You'll have to catch her first. She's buzzing around in panic and doesn't light too often. I was talking to her last night not a hundred yards removed when Guilder got it. Someone intruded on our meet. I figured maybe it was you. But now I'm thinking on a different tack. Guilder opened fire as soon as the intruder appeared, but it was a public place and anyone could have wandered in off the street—so why did he panic? I'm thinking maybe he didn't panic, maybe he knew right off who he was shooting at, and maybe he was shooting with good reason. Melissa told me that she contacted Guilder because she was scared to death and thought he could help her. But I'm wondering now . . . could Guilder have been working for Wiseman all the time you thought he was working for you?"

Cassidy's growl was reborn. "He wasn't that smart."

"Doesn't take smarts to double deal. Just the opposite. And why are you so sure Wiseman is still alive? Did you have Guilder staking out Franklin's place?"

"Whose place? The girl's?"

"No. *Charles* Franklin, the screenwriter, Melissa's husband."

Cassidy shook his head. "I never figured him for anything . . ."

"He was with Wiseman in Mexico when the horse fell on him. Claims to have been in love with Wiseman but married Melissa a year later and—"

"In love? He's gay?"

"Says he's gay but also celibate. Says he never lived with Melissa. Apparently Wiseman arranged the marriage and sent the girl off to Mexico . . ."

The old ex-cop gave me a long, hard look. "How'd you get all this shit in such a short time?"

"It's not nearly enough. You knew nothing?"

"I knew that Franklin and Melissa were married. I knew that Franklin and Wiseman were pals, made some pictures together. And I figured that Franklin knew that his pal was banging his wife. But I never heard this other stuff."

"Guilder never hinted at anything like that?"

"Not so's you'd notice."

"You definitely feel Wiseman is still alive?"

"Have to," he said. "Makes no sense any other way."

"Maybe it's not supposed to make sense. Maybe Guilder—"

"What about Guilder?"

"Ever heard of a double-wrapper? Could the New York people have sent you to watch Wiseman, then tapped Guilder to watch you? And could he have been playing a different game the whole time?"

"He was here when I came . . ."

"Made from an actor," I said. "It's Tinseltown, Butch, not the streets of New York. Everyone here is an actor—the waiters, the tailors, the candlestick makers, most all of them came out to make it in pictures or television and they end up doing what they can to survive. You don't have to be smart to act, you just have to know how to get into a role and believe it's really you. Then you can make anyone believe. So what did Guilder make you believe?"

"The son of a bitch . . ."

"Look past the false fronts and tell me what you see, Butcher."

He gave me one of his terrible smiles. "I think I better call New York."

"Do that," I said. "And when you get the man on the line, ask him if he really wants you to find Bernie Wiseman."

"I'll do that. Can I give him your regards?"

"Give him nothing. Tell him when I find Wiseman, *if* I find Wiseman, I'm going to drape him around both of your necks."

Foolish talk, Copp, as Butch was quick to point out. "Don't try to be a hero," he solemnly advised.

"You bury heroes."

"That's right."

"Loan me your car."

He dropped the keys onto the revolver. "I think maybe you'll pull it off. Mind if I just sit back and watch?"

"You've been leaning on me all the way, haven't you?"

He smiled. "Smart guys don't bust their ass."

"You're the one fed the tip-lines, sicced Edgar on me."

"Couldn't happen to a nicer, more deserving guy," he said still smiling.

"It happened to Ken Forta," I told him.

"Who's he?"

"An honest cop who died trying to unravel this. You pulled the trigger by remote control, meaning to or not. You fuzzied up this whole damned investigation, Cassidy, and the pieces haven't stopped settling yet. Who knows how many needless deaths are swimming in your pot. But that doesn't bother you, does it?"

He shrugged, nudged the gun and the keys toward me. "Just don't try to be a hero."

I was not feeling heroic at the moment. What I was feeling was *fear*—and I thought again of friend Nancy Parker's one-word message, and knew she was right.

CHAPTER TWENTY-ONE

*C*assidy's car was a Honda just like the other one, registered to UT, little silver sedan with the standard equipment and a full tank of gas—certainly no yacht but clean and capable and, one hoped, not on any hotsheets. I stopped at a 7-11 and picked up a few away-from-home necessities, then checked into a cheap Studio City motel and crashed for a few hours. I was up, bathed and shaved and on the town again before nine o'clock, went into a Denny's for their Grand Slam breakfast—pancakes and eggs, sausage and bacon, plenty of sticking power. I picked up a newspaper off the counter, thinking to catch up over coffee, caught myself staring back at me from a two-year-old photo on the front page.

The waitress had been giving me funny looks so I put the money on the counter and took the newspaper away with me—stopped at a drugstore for some heavy sunglasses and a Raider's cap, wore them out of there and to a quiet phone booth a couple blocks away.

I poked the number from Abe Johnson's poop sheet and got a first-ring response from Charlie Franklin—a cultured, "Yes?"

"Top of the morning, scribbler. Joe Copp here. We need to talk."

He sounded not pleased. "Joe, this is a—I've just been reading—you didn't tell me the police were looking for you."

I said, "I'll straighten it out after a while. Right now I'm worried about your wife. I think she's in some real danger, we need to talk about that."

"Listen, I don't want to get involved in anything that could be construed as aiding a fugitive, nothing like that, I'm sure you understand. I recommend that you turn yourself in and get a good lawyer. I could recommend one who—"

"Didn't you hear? The kid's in trouble, could be terminal. Talking to me on the telephone doesn't make you a criminal. Get off it."

". . . What can I do for you?"

"Not for me, for her. Verify a story she gave me. Was she in Mexico this whole past year or was she traipsing about glitterville with Bernie?"

"I won't discuss that."

"Don't make me come up there and shake it out of you. What does it take to get you off the fence? The girl's mangled body?"

"Joe, please . . . I am sworn to . . . let me—can you put her on the phone?"

"Wish to hell I could. But I'll go for the compromise. You call around and leave messages every place you can think of. Have her get in touch with you, quick." I gave him the number of the pay telephone. "Have her call here every hour on the hour until she connects with me."

He said, "I'll try."

"Try hard. Her life, yours too, could depend on it."

"I'll try—"

I hung up, checked the time, moved Cassidy's car to the other side of the street and half a block away, slumped in the seat and waited for . . . developments. They came pretty much as expected and in even better time than expected. An unmarked van pulled to the curb directly opposite the phone booth thirteen minutes after the mark on my watch. A man in work clothes got out and opened the side door, set some stuff on the sidewalk, got back into the van.

Uh huh.

Another van set up downrange about a block, and two unremarkable cars took station at the other end, at opposite sides of the street.

I hated to do it to the guys as much as I hate fruitless stakeouts for myself, but I needed to know. So now I knew, and since I doubted very much that there had been a tap on Franklin's phone, I was sure that sweetheart had turned me over.

I went to his house for a stakeout that I hoped would bear better fruit. It did so twenty minutes after I took station.

He came out in an S-class Mercedes, one of the big luxury sedans, and made straight for the Foothill Freeway, took an eastbound ramp. So did I.

Twenty minutes later I was wondering where in the world we were headed because we'd gone clear to the end and interchanged over to I-10, still proceeding east.

We were in Pomona, now, east even of my territory. I thought of the Ontario airport, which is international now, but we went past there, and now I was wondering just what the guy had in mind.

Then I thought of the map I had found in the UT limo, and groaned at the possibility that Palm Springs was the destination. That's a hell of a run, out past Redlands and into honest-to-God desert country, a full hour east of Ontario.

But that was where we were headed, crossing I-15, the route to Vegas, and keeping on bearing east. Understand that upper-crust Angelenos regard that whole area "out there" as their private little sandbox. When they speak of "the desert" they mean Palm Springs and environs, places like Palm Desert, Indian Wells, Cathedral City, Rancho Mirage and the whole country-club complex of exotica where nothing but sand and cactus ought to be.

It started as a hot springs oasis for the Agua Caliente Indians. Agua Caliente means "hot water," and some crafty white-eyes *cum* desert rats had vision enough a hundred years before Disney to sink some roots there. The Colorado-Sonoran desert was one of the most dreaded stretches on the old stage route between Prescott and the coast, so what better place than Agua Caliente to establish a stage stop. Later a guy named McCallum built a genuine resort called the Palm Valley Colony—that was before the turn of the century and even before Hollywood or Beverly Hills were dreamed of. But it took both Hollywood and Beverly Hills to turn Agua Caliente into the modern desert resort that it now is, and I'm talking now not sand and sagebrush but lush tropical gardens, sixty eighteen-hole golf courses, 300 tennis courts, a swimming pool for every three citizens, thirty-five miles of bicycle trails and every luxurious comfort the mind can conceive.

With all that, it's still a wasteland for me. I don't play golf or tennis, swim or lay in the sun, and I don't ride bikes in 100-plus temperatures. For ordinary people it's like Vegas without the casinos, and who the hell would go to Vegas if all the casinos closed?

But I went to Palm Springs that Friday morning because my *life* was on the line. Edgar loomed. The boys back East . . . There was never a worry about Franklin spotting the tail because the traffic never thinned once the whole distance, it's metropolitan L.A. practically all the way, desert or not, and the big problem was just keeping the Mercedes in sight as it wove eastward through the stream of cars and trucks moving hell-bent God knows where.

I even eyeballed Franklin through the final turn inside the Springs, then went on by because I had the number inscribed on my map. Really didn't know exactly what to expect there but I figured it had to be something worth the drive, and who knew?—maybe I'd even find a living dead man there.

It was a country-club-style condo complex in one of the posher areas of new development; very few of these people actually lived here more than a few months out of the year, many probably didn't see the place more than once or twice a year. It was a status symbol in certain circles to have a condo in the Springs. You didn't have to use it, you could let your friends use it and talk about it to their friends, and it looked good on the financial statement.

Please don't mind me grousing off about this sort of thing. We've got this homeless problem in L.A., you know, New York isn't the only one, thousands of indigents living on the damned sidewalks, and it burns me a little to think about all those empty condos and all the money that keeps them that way.

I left the Honda on the downside and walked back in the noonday sun, the house number on the map now etched between my ears, but I didn't need it. The Mercedes was in the drive, the garage door was open and a pretty red Jaguar with PAID DUES plates was nestled inside.

I hit the front door with a heavy foot and walked right in.

Franklin turned to face me from a picture window overlooking a golf course. "Jesus Christ . . ."

"Not even close," I said. "The name is Copp. Trot the lady out, I've come to play."

He was caught between fight and flight, weighing both, finally opting for neither. The shoulders slumped. "She's not here."

"Car's here."

"Probably out on the course," he said. "Look, let's settle this and get out before she returns. She's got enough to worry about without—"

"So why'd you come?"

"You sent me, damn it."

"Why didn't you just call?"

His attention skittered away from my gaze, the hands clenched. "Go to hell, you—"

"Jail, you mean. Didn't work, as you see. I figured you'd turn me over. But why did you? Not because you're such a law-abiding citizen. Huh?"

"Get screwed."

"Tch. I could give you a story treatment on that one, but why don't you give me one instead? A *straight* one, this time. Start with Bernie and that little accident in Mexico—"

"Please get out of here, Copp."

"Sorry, can't do that. Maybe you're a nice guy, I don't know. Right now, I can't care. Too many people seem to be after my ass. Start with Bernie. He faked the accident, somehow faked out the doctors, and now he thinks he's home clean. He's not. I'm here to tell you he's not. Because some very mean fellows have not been faked out. They know he's alive and they know he's got their money. They won't quit until they get it back. They'll kill you, they'll kill Melissa, and they'll kill everybody in their way until they do get it back. So maybe we should just start with the fifty mil. Let's take it home."

"Jesus, I don't know what you're talking about."

"Somebody around here does, so let's just sit down and get comfortable and wait for someone to get back."

But someone was already back.

She had come up softly behind me and placed the muzzle of a pistol at the base of my skull. I could hear the action as she pulled back the hammer and I even caught a glimpse of her through red haze as I turned and the gun boomed.

She was tall, and tanned, and blond—raw naked and soaking wet from tub or shower, maybe pool or Jacuzzi, who cared? I just went by-by with the crazy thought that I had died with a naked living doll etched onto my retinas and the sound of gunfire in my ears, so maybe there was a God after all.

I wasn't dead, of course. But maybe I'd have settled for that when I came out of it.

CHAPTER TWENTY-TWO

I woke up first in the trunk of a moving car. I was hogtied and had the taste of blood in my mouth, my eyes were matted with it dry and sticky, and I had a headache that could be described only with kettledrums and crashing cymbals. My ears rang. I welcomed the black waves that kept washing in on me.

So I guess I was in and out a lot, or maybe it just seemed a lot or it was mixed with dreams. There were a lot of people around, in and out, and voices tumbling about, all distorted in my ringing ears. I have memories—dreams or otherwise—of bouncing along a rough road in the trunk of a car, red-fogged visions of an Indian boy and a tall blond beauty, of the doggy boy, the VW, and distorted faces I thought I should recognize but didn't.

Maybe I actually saw a wheelchair somewhere,

and I think for certain I saw the dry-wash ravine and felt myself sliding into it.

I heard a rattler and felt myself frying in the sun; I remember a group of dark-skinned people peering down at me and another Indian boy with a sweatband around his head, and I felt the hands that lifted me up and carried me away.

The first lucid moment oriented me to the night sky through a window with no glass in it. I was lying on a makeshift bed. Two Indian women were sponging my body with a cool liquid. They shushed me when I tried to speak, and one of them went to get the men.

There were three of those, one very old and obviously in charge. He smiled at me and said, "Did you decide to keep the body?"

"Is it worth anything?" My voice was a croak.

"Only to you, I guess. Someone tossed it away like an empty skin. But it will mend, I think it will mend and walk again."

I said, "That's nice, I guess," and that's all I remember of that.

I woke up next time in muted daylight, covered with a light blanket and lying facedown, my face in some sort of soft yoke. Someone was doing things to the back of my head—sponging it with a liquid, I think. Whatever, it felt good. The ringing and the drums and cymbals were gone, but my mouth tasted like I'd gone to sleep with a dead mouse in it. I heard the murmur of voices outside or in another room.

I tried to lift my head, decided against it, but I guess the attempt provoked a response from my nurse. She moved quickly away, and again the old man came to see me.

He helped me turn over and sit upright, then gave

me water—mixed with a little whiskey, I think. "You're fine, fine. Don't worry. You are in good hands. My granddaughters make excellent medicine and they attend you night and day. Am I mistaken or do you prefer this to an emergency room and curious policemen?"

It wasn't easy to talk but I told him, "I think you're right, grandfather. Unless there's a bullet in my head. Is there?"

"Oh I think it missed by maybe two of your hairs. Never mind, there are plenty of hairs left and they will grow over the ditch in your scalp. Do you have dizziness?"

Sure I had dizziness. "I appreciate what you've done, friend. But I've got to get moving as soon as I can. How soon would you say?"

"Tomorrow. Meanwhile, do not worry."

"What day is this?"

"This day is Sunday."

"Morning or evening?"

"Morning. You have been two nights with us."

"Am I on the reservation?"

"Yes."

"Don't you want to know how I got here?"

"Oh, we brought you here. My grandson saw them drop you into the ravine. Why they did that to you, it is your business not mine unless you want to make it mine."

I said, "This business you don't need, friend. And I need to take it off your doorstep. So if you'll just get my clothes and help me find my feet . . ."

Don't get the idea that I was in a tepee. The Aguas are not poor. They still own much of the developed land in the area and have kept the best for their own use. Landlords to the rich, if you will. Some of the Palm Springs incorporated areas are still Indian lands.

The kid who found me was only five years old. He and an older brother were playing and he was lying on top of a rock and scouting white-eyes when a shiny car appeared and "white people" pulled another gringo from the trunk and dropped him into a shallow ravine. I was bloody, powder-burned and I guess a scary sight to the kids, but they ran for help and the whole family responded.

Grandfather's name was Emilio, a fine gentleman in my book. The Indians have their own style of dignity. I'll take it over the corporate jungle anytime anywhere. These people still manage to have their feet on the earth and their hands in the stars, and they say that the human being is the natural conduit between the two. They think of themselves that way, I guess—especially those who still remember the old ways. I'll never argue with it.

The women had restored my clothes to almost good as new—even got the bloodstains out—and not an item was missing from my pockets. The gunleather was intact, pistol all cleaned and oiled, loaded and ready to fire. I had a burned groove in my lower scalp a quarter-inch wide and two inches long, clear to the bone and whittling a bit. The way Emilio described the wound when he first saw it, my gringo friends probably thought that the bullet had pierced the skull and jellied some brain tissue. They tossed me away to die, and maybe I would have anyway if the kid hadn't spotted me.

It took me all that day to get my walking legs back. Emilio and his sons drove me into town at sundown and we found the Honda just as I had left it two days earlier. I thanked them again, we shook hands all around, they went back to the reservation.

I was still a bit light in the head but able to return to the scene of the crime. I parked the Honda in the driveway and rang the doorbell, got no response, went around and peered through the picture window, saw no signs of life in there; went to the office and made a gentle inquiry.

They had no Franklin in their complex, no Wiseman or Moore; I could get that much but no crossreference by number, that was a no-no.

I didn't want to push my luck so I got the hell out. I still felt poorly and wanted the soft touch and gentle hands of an understanding woman; I wanted the sanctuary of Nancy Parker's apartment.

The drive back to L.A. was practically a meditation, punctuated by mental kicks in the ass and a growingly cynical attitude towards the human situation, the gringo humans anyway. But I knew I'd never make it as an Indian, the genes just aren't there, and besides I hate the fucking desert. Face it, I like where people are, great hordes of people all butting and shoving against one another, competing for the buck and for standing room on a growingly crowded planet—it's what I was born to.

I finally admitted to myself that I like it, and that by God nobody was going to shove me off of my turf. I lost my fear, in that moment of honesty, because I suddenly realized who I am.

I'm Joe Copp, by God I'm big and I'm mean and I can take care of business with the best of them. I'm just as smart and just as capable as any son of a bitch when I'm in my own, and I'm in my own when I'm doing what I know is right.

No son of a bitch is going to bleed my friends. Not as long as I have breath in the lungs and fire in the head.

I'm bad Joe Copp and I'm burning all over with the need to take it back to those of sonofbitches.

Fuck sanctuary, I wanted blood.

CHAPTER TWENTY-THREE

It required some fancy footwork but I ran down Abe Johnson's home address and presented myself to him at ten o'clock that night.

He stood framed in his open doorway, a big powerful-looking man with commanding shoulders that nearly filled the opening. He grabbed me and pulled me inside. "For God's sake, man, what are you *doing* here?"

I said, "Sorry to bring it home to you, Abe, but we've just got to talk."

I don't know how many emotions washed over that big black face as he stood there contemplating a fugitive in his living room. It was a modest ranch style in one of the newer subdivisions in the north valley, comfortably furnished and neat as a pin except for a kid's toy here and there. A playpen occupied the center of the room and a television murmured at us from somewhere out of view.

A child's voice yelled from the back. "Mummy..."

I said, "God, Abe, I'm really sorry but—"

Angela came into the room and relieved the awkwardness. She looked great in a lounge robe and white socks, a bit thicker in the middle than I remembered but just as pretty. She said, "Abe—" then saw me and caught herself. "The kids want you to tuck them in."

He gave me a grim look and patted his wife's arm as he left the room.

I said, "You look great, Angie."

"Can't say the same for you, Joe. You look as usual. How long since you've been to bed? For sleeping, I mean."

That was a shot. I took it with a smile. "I'm really happy for you, mummy."

She smiled back. "I'm plenty happy enough for myself, but thanks. They're great kids."

"Have to be."

She came over and hugged me at the arms. "Joe, Joe—what's going to become of you? Still chasing dragons and tilting at windmills. Aren't you getting a little old for that kind of stuff?"

It had been a lot of years, but at that moment they were all wiped away. I kissed her forehead and she raised a hand to the back of my neck like she used to do. I winced and pulled away from that. She quickly dropped the hand. "My God, what's that you've got back there?"

"Small hurt," I told her. "It's healing."

Abe was back. He came over and pulled me around, checked out the damage.

"Headshot," I muttered. "Got lucky. It went around instead of through."

He said, "You need to get that to a doctor."

"It's been to the best," I assured him.

"Why isn't it bandaged?"

"It is bandaged. Nature's way, they said. Never mind that. We've got to talk."

"I'll put on some coffee," Angela said, and left us alone.

Abe asked me in a quietly furious voice, "How could you bring this here, Joe?"

"Had no place else to take it, Abe."

He took me back to the eat-in kitchen and we sat and stared at each other across the table while Angela banged around with a coffeepot. Presently he said, "Okay, start talking."

"You first," I said. "How'd you make out after that dumb-ass stunt on the telephone?"

"I've been reassigned," he replied soberly. "Community relations." He smiled, at something on my face, I guess, and added, "Pending a full review. It's okay, I think of it as a vacation. I'll be on sane hours for a while and maybe I'll get reacquainted with my kids. Now you."

"Still you. What's happening with the case?"

"I told you. I'm reassigned. Don't know and don't really care what's happening with the case."

Angela plugged in the coffeepot and left in response to another summons from the kids' bedroom. Abe's eyes followed her out, then he turned to me. "That's a good woman, Joe. We have her in common, you and me, both loved by Angela. Why does something like that always seem to drive men apart instead of bringing them closer together?"

I said, "I feel as close to you as any man I've ever known, and I don't really know you. And you went overboard for me, pal, without being asked. So I guess the logic doesn't apply to us."

"Sure it does. I don't really know you either, and I'm not even sure I like you. I don't like to look at you and get a picture of Angela lying in your arms. But I love her, and so I honor her love for others. I just want you to know, that's where you stand with me. Anything you get from me, you get because of Angela."

She came back in at that moment, caught us staring at each other and picked up on the feelings there, I guess. "You guys talking about me?"

Abe told her, "Now don't you have a high opinion of yourself . . . why would us two cops be discussing a tired old housewife going into middle-age spread?"

She made a mock swing at him and said from the doorway, "Watch the coffee. I'm watching TV."

He blew her a kiss, and that big beautiful smile faded as he turned back to me. "What I'm telling you, man, is that you're still affecting her life. So just how do you want me to play it?"

I stood up. "You've played it enough. I appreciate it, whatever the reason."

"Use the back door," he said.

He went out with me and we stood in the darkness back there. He told me, "They're still dying, Joe. That man Cassidy was blown out of his bed Saturday morning. Today they fished a body out of the Hollywood reservoir and it's been identified as a woman who worked for Justine Wiseman. Maybe Mrs. Wiseman is dead somewhere, too, because she's disappeared without a trace. What the hell is going on here?"

I replied, "You just said it, without a trace. That's what they're doing, removing all traces."

"What *who* is doing?"

"They. I don't have a real make on *they* yet. Is the dead woman a young Mexican girl?"

"No, a physical-fitness coach. She lived with—"

"Viking Woman," I said.

"Her name was Hulda Swenson. She lived with Justine Wiseman. Her mother was Bernie Wiseman's housekeeper."

My new wound was beginning to throb again. I told Abe: "I think Wiseman's still alive. I also think he stole fifty million from his company. I think Charlie and Melissa Franklin somehow helped him set it up. I don't think he had an accident in Mexico. I don't think he needs a wheelchair. I don't know who died in that blast, but I think the evidence was rigged. I think they rigged me into it partly to confuse the picture further. I think they headshot all those people as further confusion. To make it look like mob executions. People back East pulling strings, etcetera. I found a condo in Palm Springs where someone's been lying low. That's where I got shot. They thought I was dead or dying and dumped me in a desert ravine. That was Friday. Some Indians found me and doctored me. I knew from nothing until today."

"What's the address of that condo?"

I handed it to him on a slip of paper already made out. "I'm too hot to run a make. I thought maybe you could do that. Also try to get a line on a place down near San Quintin in Baja, supposedly owned or maybe leased by Wiseman. Melissa Franklin told me she spent the whole past year down there but I don't know, I sniff more staged confusion there. Charlie Franklin is deep into this, I don't know how dirty but certainly deep inside of it. He's the one led me to Palm Springs. There's another guy, posed as Wiseman's chauffeur the day they came out to my place. He's about the same general description as Albert Moore. I saw him at Justine's place on Thursday night, playing sex games for a party of gay women. If you've got another John Doe with a tag on the toe, you might try that connection—I'd say he's a hot candidate for it."

He commented, "You've been a busy boy."

I handed him another slip of paper. "These are license tags I jotted down in Justine's driveway Thursday night. The way they all ran, I'd guess a little discreet pressure would produce quick cooperation. Most of these women are probably married to important men who would shit and go blind if the truth came out."

"This was a gay party?"

"Yeah, your physical culturist acted like head dyke around there. I think probably Justine can go either way and switches with opportunity and mood. She's tough as nails, so—"

"Tell me about it," Johnson said.

I said, "That's all I have. Oh . . . Butch Cassidy told me early Friday morning that his sponsors in New York were eager to make a deal with Wiseman to get their money back. He made it sound like forgive and forget."

"His sponsors are syndicate people?"

"Sounds like, yeah. This Klein is, I gather, their financial minister. But I don't think they're actively behind any of what's going down out here. Cassidy told me that he'd been watching Wiseman for a year, that he finally nailed the evidence—a secret set of books—and took it East just a week ago—well, a week ago when he told me. According to Cassidy their reaction was to play it cool, find the money first. What would happen next is not too hard to figure out, but somehow I think the bloodletting is mostly Wiseman's fancy footwork erasing the tracks and confusing the picture. Remember, he's a bright boy.

He's obviously been playing footsie with these fellows for years—maybe even before he came out from New York—so he must know the rules of play. I think it's significant, though, that the hell all started coming down after Cassidy busted the play."

"You should have stayed with the force, Joe," Abe said.

"I never fit into that. Ask Angela, she knows what a jerk I am."

"She told me," he said.

"It's why she left me. Told me that cowboys make lousy lovers and even lousier husbands."

"You're not a cowboy."

"Sure I am. Don't disillusion me."

I shook his hand, asked him to make my good-by to Angela. He told me: "Hang onto your ass, Zorro. Keep in touch. I'll try to feed you."

"Forget it, I just fed you. Now I'm finished feeding. I'm going for blood."

"Carefully."

Sure. And I knew just where I wanted to start.

CHAPTER TWENTY-FOUR

I needed no fancy footwork to find this guy. He lived the same place he had lived for thirty years, one of the charming old homes in the foothill college community of Claremont, lived there as a kid and inherited the place when his folks died. Never married, never had a girl as far as I knew—Edgar had always been a strange man with strange ways and weird friends. I had played poker a couple of times in this house, went back the second time out of sheer charity, never knew anyone else who went back more than once.

He's not much good at anything, Edgar isn't, except department politics. For that, he's a natural—kind of guy who laughs only at the discomfort of others and sneers at every man's success. A weird little prick and I'd always despised his guts.

The feeling, of course, was entirely mutual, which

didn't make me special. Edgar, I think, despised everybody.

He answered the bell with the door on a security chain, showed only his nose to ask, "Who's there?"

"It's Joe Copp."

He bounced it off the chain and came out in his stocking feet and pants, nothing else except his service revolver leading the way.

Edgar had never been hard, but now it was ridiculous. A couple years younger than me, about five-ten and one-seventy to one-eighty, too much beer and too much television over too many years had given him a potbelly and sagging tits. He was near bald, too, and looked fifty years old if a day.

I told him the truth: "You look like shit, Edgar."

"Shut up." He jabbed the gun at me. "Against the wall. You're under arrest."

"Big deal."

He was fumbling at his hip pocket for a pair of cuffs, too anxious for the collar, when I kneed him in the groin and took his pistol.

He fell back into the house, curled up like a fetus. I closed the door and unloaded his pistol, tossed it into a chair, threw the bullets to the other side of the room. I picked him up by his belt and deposited him on the couch. "Learn a little humility."

"Rotten—"

"Look who's calling what rotten, the guy who went to bed with Butch Cassidy. Shall we call you Sundance now, prick?"

"You're crazy."

"You're the one that's crazy, going to bed with a guy like that. He's mob-connected all the way. You're lucky someone blew him out of his skin, else he'd have his hooks in you the rest of your life. What a dumbo you are."

I almost literally had the opponent by the balls. I prodded a fat buttock with my knee. "It was a setup going in, wasn't it?—and I played right into it. Actually I'm the dumbo, you're the smart one, I'm the fool who's got cops chasing his ass. I don't like that, Edgar. I *resent* that."

"Joe, I didn't set you up. I already had the video when the guy came to me. Hey, he worked for Wiseman and he said the guy was still alive. He said L.A. was booting it, and he offered to work with me to straighten it out."

"He was your tipster?"

"Well, yeah, but . . . it made sense. And we heard your name mentioned a couple of times on the audio side of the tape."

"Mentioned how?"

"Copp, just Copp."

"Did they spell it for you, Edgar?"

"It could've been either way. I had to take the worst case."

"Or the best for you?"

"Cassidy suggested we put the pressure on you and see which way you ran."

"So, of course, you being such a cooperative officer of the law, you reluctantly took the advice of a security sister from the private sector to put the screws to a former officer—"

"Okay, so I didn't mind it all that much. But I didn't set you up—"

"You knew damned well I hadn't committed any crime—"

"I knew nothing. What the hell, you've been out of

the department a long time. How the hell do I know what you're up to these days?"

"My worst enemies could tell you."

"Joe, I *didn't* set you up."

I toed him in the butt. "Where has your investigation taken you?"

"Guess it's sort of stalled."

"I guess it is. And the bodies are still falling while you help play helter-skelter in a chase for an innocent. Namely *me . . .*"

"It was L.A. put out the APB. I tried to tell 'em—"

"Tried to tell 'em what?"

"That you'd come home."

"You dumb ass, the last time I went home I found Forta and Rodriguez decorating with their own blood. What do you think we're doing here? You think all of this was designed in heaven to get you a shitface promotion? Damn near two dozen people are dead. I've been conked and headshot myself, and that's only the easiest part. Why are you lounging around watching television and drinking beer when two of your deputies are fresh in their graves? Why aren't you out there looking for the reason? Where was your great victory just now when you thought you were going to put the cuffs on me? The cop that caught terrible Joe Copp? Big deal. I haven't killed anybody, I haven't plotted against anybody. You know it as well as I know it. So what kind of dumbshit games are we playing here, Edgar? Damn you, *tell* me."

The guy actually started to shake. Whether from pain or rage I couldn't say, but it was all I was going to get from him, so I got the hell out.

At least he was a good warm-up for the night I had in mind.

* * *

She couldn't have been more than nineteen or twenty, maybe less, with one of those dreamshine complexions without cosmetics and frightened eyes. Or maybe she just looked that way when I was around.

"No hay nadie aqui," she told me at the door, then repeated it in tremulous English: "There is no one here."

I believed she comprehended the lingo better than she sometimes let on, a natural defense.

I went on in. "You're here." She didn't react to that so I tried it in her lingo, though I have a bad time with Spanish syntax. *"Aqui usted."*

She showed me an almost smile. *"Si, por . . .* and that's all I got of that so I decided I'd better quit showing off and stick to English.

"Let me see your Green Card," I said, a dirty trick because I well knew she could not produce one. L.A. is overrun with illegals and she fit the profile.

Of course she just gave me the patented blank look that all the border smugglers must teach to their illegals. It can cover many embarrassing moments.

I told her, "Forget it, I'm kidding, it's okay."

"Okay?"

"Yeah, *comprende?* No card, okay."

"No card okay."

"You got it."

She showed me a dazzling smile. *"Gracias."*

"Nada. Where's your boss?"

She pumped her shoulders. "Boss leave Friday, say back Monday. Police come today, say—"

"They tell you about Hulda?"

"Yes."

"Did they come in and search?"

"Search? Yes. Her room."

"Where is that?"

She looked toward the gym. "There."

"Next to Mrs. Wiseman's rooms?"

"Yes."

"Where is your room?"

She looked to the other direction.

"Near the kitchen?"

"Yes."

"You were a knockout Thursday night."

She put a questioning hand to her breast. "Knock-out?"

"You, beautiful. *Muy guapa.*"

Color flooded into her cheekbones and her eyes went to the floor. Great eyes. You've maybe noticed that I have a thing about eyes. This kid had it, all of it . . . "Sorry, didn't mean to embarrass you."

"I must dress as I am told."

I said, "It's okay with me. I meant it. You looked great."

She gave me the damnedest coquette look and said very softly, *"Gracias."*

"Like your job?"

"Yes."

"Get along with Mrs. Wiseman okay?"

"Yes."

"And Hulda?"

"Yes."

"Even when they hit on you?"

"Hit? No. Never hit."

"I meant . . . never mind. I'd like to see Hulda's room."

She led me to it, through the gym and the bath obviously shared with the lady of the house—a large room at the rear, surprisingly feminine and subtly attractive.

"Do you have a name?"

"My name is Carmencita."

"Could you get me something to drink?"

"Coke? Whiskey?"

"Coke is fine. In a glass, please. With ice. And could you bring some extra ice?"

"Extra?"

"In a towel."

She gave me a puzzled look but went to fill the request.

I immediately violated Hulda's privacy, figuring she didn't need it anymore anyway.

The clothing, like the room, was surprisingly feminine, and the intimate apparel was even more so. Not a lot of it, but what was there was Rodeo Drive quality and tastefully attractive. The cop who had searched ahead of me had obviously been in a hurry. The only drawers that looked disturbed were the deeper ones with layers of clothing; in these the stuff had been tossed about some and obviously displaced. In a shallower drawer a small photo album lay concealed and probably unnoticed beneath bundles of athletic socks.

The cop must have hurried right past that drawer without feeling for treasures below. I did not, and I came up with treasures indeed, I hoped.

Most of the photos showed scenes and people that meant nothing, five did. There was one of Hulda and her smiling mother, Edda—a fairly recent Polaroid taken in the kitchen of the Bel Air cottage. Another showed Edda barely in the picture and looking rather wistfully toward a man in a wheelchair, and the man looking into the camera. Still another had the man in the wheelchair and Justine Wiseman on his lap, both smiling into the camera. The other two were variations on the same subjects. All five were Polaroids and seemed to have been taken at about the same time.

I noticed that five of the plastic envelopes in the series were empty. Seemed to me that Polaroid film packs come ten shots to the pack. I wondered if someone had removed five of the shots from that album, and, if so, why.

Anyway I lifted the other five and put the album back.

Carmencita returned with a tray. I sat on the bed and made an ice necklace with the towel, draped it around the back of my head, which was hurting. The kid made sympathy noises and moved around to kneel behind me and help with the application.

So I sat there and let her do it, sipped coke and thought unacceptable thoughts while the kid ministered to my hurts.

After a moment she said, "I understand now what is mean by hit on. Hulda, yes. Mrs. Wiseman, no. Mrs. Wiseman tell Hulda, 'Leave the maid alone.' So she did. But sometimes . . ."

"Sometimes she didn't."

"Yes. Sometimes I wake up in the night and see Hulda at my door, and she calls my name. I do not answer, and she goes away."

I told her, "Love is hard all over . . . look how tough it gets in the usual ways, think how much worse it must get for the other ones."

She replied, "Yes. I see this many times here. It is sad. Is it sad?"

"Yeah, kid, it's very sad."

We had become pals.

I reminded her, "The party Thursday night. *Jueves noche.* You were Frenchy frilly. Ooh-la-la."

She giggled softly, nodded.

"There were two men here. *Hombres.*"

"Yes. And you."

"And me, yes. One wore a dog collar."

"Roberto."

"Roberto? Not *Al*berto?"

"No, Roberto. He is much here. He is known to Mrs. Wiseman."

"Know his full name?"

"No."

"Know where he lives?"

"No. I think he—"

"It's important, *muy importa.*"

"I think maybe he too is a friend of Mr. Franklin."

"Franklin? Did he come around here much?"

"No, not since—oh, maybe—yes, he is here."

"Socially?"

"Sometimes, yes. He is a good friend with Señor Wiseman. No?"

"Yes, but—"

"Roberto I think works for Mr. Franklin. He is, what you say?—handyman?"

"And he comes here socially with his boss?"

"Oh no, socially no." She giggled again. "For the parties, yes, but socially no." She touched the crown of my head lightly with delicate fingers. "Is better now?"

"A thousand times better. I stood up and gave her

my hand, helped her off the bed, then went in and shook down Justine's room and found a few more treasures—I hoped.

Carmencita was standing at Hulda's window with a solemn face when I went back to her.

I asked, "Do you have any people in the area?"

"People?"

"Familia."

"Oh yes, I have an uncle."

"Where?"

"He lives in Baldwin Park."

"You're in luck. That's on my way. Get your things, I'm taking you home."

"Oh *no, Señora* Wiseman returns tomorrow—"

"Great. If she does, then you can return the day after tomorrow. But I can't leave you here, kid. You're so much raw meat."

"Por que?"

"Raw meat. Like Hulda." Her eyes became very large. "Maybe. Don't get scared, just cautious. And now go get your things."

She walked out of there very slowly, looking over her shoulder at me as though hoping I would call her back.

I couldn't do that.

I knew how she felt. Probably supporting a whole extended family in Mexico from her salary as a maid for the rich and famous. Not that the bread came so heavy here, not even from the rich and famous, but because so very little went so very far down there. But I couldn't cancel the order because that might be the same as cancelling the kid, and she was much too good to waste.

She came back with a cardboard suitcase and I

took her home to Uncle Francisco in Baldwin Park. A considerable contrast to San Marino. Hellish conditions.

It was not that far out of my way, in more ways than one . . . I was already halfway to hell myself.

I pulled up at the guard shack and killed the engine, dropped the keys into the guy's hand. He gave me a look and asked, "What's this?"

I flashed the ID at him. "Returning Cassidy's car."

"Cassidy died yesterday."

I said, "That's why the delivery service. It's a studio car."

"Well don't leave it here."

"Where do you want it?"

He gave me back the keys and told me how to find the security building. "Leave it around back."

"Whatever you say," I told him, and meant it because that was where I'd wanted to go all along and I didn't have a card to actuate the employee gate.

He made note of the license tag. "Just leave the keys in it. I'll report it. Unless you want me to sign a—"

I smiled and waved him away. He smiled back and waved me on through.

I put the car in a security slot behind the building and let myself into the office using Cassidy's keys. All was neat and clean in there, silent, abandoned. I sat at the desk and went through drawers, hoping I was ahead of the cops on this one, but found nothing that meant anything to me.

A small combination safe with correspondence stacked on top of it sat beside the desk. It was locked.

The correspondence was routine stuff, some of it very old. I sympathized with Cassidy's filing system: just leave the stuff where you can see it, then you'll never have a problem finding it. These letters had been scattered all over the top of the desk the last time I'd been in there.

I pulled out desk drawers one by one again and explored their undersides by touch, scored on the third try and pulled off a small index card taped to it. It was the combination.

I found some treasure in the safe, but it was going to take a while to put it together in any meaningful pattern. It was all neatly boxed and ready to go so I took it and went, left everything else the way I'd found it.

I exited via the automatic gates on the employee lot, didn't need a card to get out, could hardly wait to find somewhere cool and go through the treasure trove at a leisurely pace.

There was a videocassette in that box, Xerox copies of various legal documents, package of still photographs, a small spiral notebook crammed with cryptic notations in some personal brand of shorthand and a complete medical history on Bernard Wiseman.

I figured it was Cassidy's case file.

And I surely wanted to know what Butch had known that got him killed.

I did not find it in such precise terms. But I found the pointers, and for the moment the pointers were enough.

I found, for example, evidence to suggest that Wiseman had been doing illicit business of some sort with *NuCal Designs,* paying them on studio vouchers for services that had never been performed.

I found also that *NuCal* was involved in more than costume design. They also did graphic design and special effects. I already knew that one of the dead partners had been a respected film editor. Now I learned that the other one had been a freelance acting coach specializing in dialogue training, which usually meant emphasis on foreign and regional speech, accents and the like. Cassidy also believed that the background operation was pirating porno flicks for bootleg videocassette sales out the back door, lately a booming enterprise in the area. Nickel-and-dime stuff, to be sure, but those fives and tens add up.

Wiseman had a piece of the action.

So did his wife, Justine.

One of the legal papers in the file was a separate agreement between the Wisemans and the official partners in *NuCal* broadly spelling out the business arrangements. The Wisemans jointly held a one-third interest.

There was also an interesting angle on Justine herself. Apparently Wiseman had hired a private dick to spy on her shortly after their breakup. The packet of photos was a pictorial backup to the dick's pithy summary: "Subject exhibits an unrestrained sexual appetite, appears to be sexually addicted."

Who isn't sexually addicted to one degree or another, to one thing or another, but it's one of the new buzzwords in psychiatry, and the meaning was quite clear. Wiseman had been gathering evidence to fight his wife in court.

As for Bernie's medical file—I had to swallow hard on that one because I'd already decided that he'd faked the accident in Mexico. This record started in Mexico and it gave a blow-by-blow description of all the damage sustained in that accident, complete with X rays and sonograms, a follow-up with local doctors confirming the Mexican prognosis: the patient would never walk again.

I got all that in the quick scan.

I needed time to study it all more closely, to skull the thing a bit, but figured I didn't have that kind of time up front.

By my educated guess a few too many people were still alive and the clock was running down on them. Besides, I'd reached full heat.

So I went back to Glendale, one more time.

CHAPTER TWENTY-FIVE

It was nearly midnight when I reached the hills of Franklin's neighborhood. His house was dark except for patio lights. A small sports car stood in the drive, an MG I thought. Two guys were standing alongside and putting things in it when I drove up.

I blocked the drive broadside and hit the pavement, gun in hand.

"Uh uh," I said, because they'd taken one look at me and apparently had decided to run.

Both were mid-twenties, handsome and well built. Well built all over, I knew, because I'd seen them both before, naked.

"Taking off?" I asked Roberto.

He was in a sweat, eyes on the gun in my hand, frozen. Same guy, yeah, who'd parked a limo at my office door and told me, "Mr. Moore would like to talk to you."

This time the poise was gone. "Yeah, uh—we, we're just leaving. Charlie's not here—"

"Not looking for Charlie here, pal. Looking for you."

The other one quickly told me, "Hey, I got nothing in this. I don't know what the beef is but—"

"Haven't I seen you at Chippendale's?" I asked him, only kidding of course.

He said, "No, you saw me at San Marino the other night."

"Right," I said, dramatically cocking a finger at him. "You were trying to get between a couple of Siamese sisters. How did it turn out?"

He actually giggled and gave a quick look at his partner. "Only way it can when I'm not writing the script. How'd yours turn?"

I told him, "Wrote my own script and put her on her ass."

He laughed. "I wanted to stay and see that."

The other one said, "Tony, shut up," then asked me, "What do you want?"

"I want you to make me a bomb."

He stared at me very soberly for a long moment. "I don't know how to make a bomb."

"Sure you do. Anyway, I brought you the book." I flipped it out of my coat—one of those mimeographed paperbacks from an underground press—showed it to him, put it back. "Justine loaned it to me."

"I never saw that before, I don't know what you're talking about—"

"Let's go take a look at your workshop. Maybe that will revive your memory."

He said, "Listen—"

"You listen. The whole thing is nailed and the cops

are probably on their way here right now. You can stonewall it clear into the gas chamber for all I care. We can just stand here and wait for them or—"

"What the hell is this?" the other one yelled.

Roberto said, "Shut up, Tony."

I said, "Yeah, Tony, shut up. This guy doesn't care about your neck. I'd say his interest ends at your ass."

"Bull," said Tony. "He's never had my ass. I don't use it that way. I just want it very clear that I don't know from nothing here, I got no part of it."

I told him, "Maybe you didn't write the script, pal, but you've sure got a part in it. How are you with death scenes?"

Tony looked to Roberto again. "What's he *talking* about?"

"Shut up," said the part-time chauffeur.

"Yeah," I said, "let's all shut up and just stand here and wait. It's okay. I don't know about you two, but I've got all night. Nice view up here, isn't it."

"I wanta know, *what* death scenes?"

"It's a big cast," I told the curious Tony. "Everybody dies in the end. All the dumb ones die. Like Roberto and you. Only the stars survive, as usual."

Roberto was beginning to crumble. A siren sounded in the distance, probably down on the freeway, nothing to do with us but he couldn't be sure of that.

Tony grabbed him by the arm. "What's he *talking* about, Robbie? Did you build a bomb for somebody? Dammit, I told you—"

"Shut *up,*" Roberto screeched.

I shoved him toward the gate to the patio, shoved the other one too, told them both, "Let's go find the lab."

"All right, wait," Roberto wailed. "What do you want?"

"I want my ass back," I told him.

"Okay, I drove the car. But I didn't wire it."

"Who did?"

"I don't know, I guess Albert did. We just changed places for a while, that's all. And that's all I know about it."

"Why change?"

"I wasn't told why. I just drove the man to the meeting with you."

"That was Monday. What about Tuesday?"

"Okay, I had the car for only a few minutes Tuesday. Just long enough to meet you and pick up the film. We changed off after that and I took the other limo back to the lot."

"What lot?"

"The studio lot."

"Who else was in the limo when you took it back to the studio?"

"Nobody else."

"Where was the man?"

"He was in the other limo."

"All that time?"

"Well, no, not all that time I had it. We were changing around back and forth."

"Why?"

"Hell, I don't know why. They just didn't want you to know who you were dealing with, I guess."

"Why the big shell game with the cars?"

"I don't . . . same reason, I guess."

"Where was the wheelchair?"

"What wheelchair?"

"What wheelchair do you think?"

"I don't know. It was in the limo, last I saw it."

"Which limo?"

"For God's sake, what difference does it make?"

"A lot, because the one limo was designed for the wheelchair and the other wasn't. So where did you last see it?"

He seemed to be trying to remember, finally said, "I think it was in the studio limo because I remember Albert carrying him. I know at least once I saw Albert carrying him between the cars."

"Go back to Monday," I said. "You drove the man and the lady out to my place."

"I told you that."

"Same man?"

"Well, sure."

"Who was the lady?"

"She looked like Mrs. Wiseman."

"Looked like?"

"Well, yes, but not exactly."

"Don't play with me. I might look sweet but you know what they say about looks . . ."

"I'm not playing with you. And you don't look sweet to me."

"No? I'm destroyed. This is my sweet face. How long you been with Franklin?"

"A couple of months."

"Then you never met his wife?"

"Didn't know he had one." He looked a bit hurt.

"How much do you know about Franklin?"

"Not much. Nice guy, pays well, doesn't ask for much."

"Ever wonder why you're around?"

"I know why I'm around. He likes me."

"Wonderful. I like you too. Would that make you want to blow up something for me?"

He cast a wise look at his pal as he replied, "Depends on what you want blown and how big it is."

I waggled the gun at him. "Blow on this, guy."

Tony had been staring at his friend with great interest from the beginning of the exchange. Now he interrupted. "Let's do a movie on this. This is really far out. By the way, what man are we talking about?"

"Just shut *up,*" Roberto told him. "Stay out of it. You got no piece of it, remember?"

"Up yours, you little queer," said Tony right back.

"Good question, though," I said. "How would you answer it, Roberto? Who is the man?"

"I guess it was Wiseman," he said quietly.

"You guess."

"Well, okay, it was him."

"The real McCoy? Or the real decoy?"

"I thought it was him."

"Still think it was?"

"How do I know? All I did was drive the car. Wish I'd never seen the damned thing. A hundred bucks, a lousy hundred bucks. I'd give them a hundred of my own to take it all back. This has been a nightmare for me, man. A nightmare. Doesn't that mean anything to you?"

"Maybe it should," I said. "Maybe you were just a bystander like me. If that's true, then it'll all come out in the wash. If not . . . well, kiddo, it's people like you they invented gas chambers for."

Tony fairly shivered. "I think it'd make a hell of a picture," he said seriously.

"Shut up," Roberto instructed.

Which brought the expected response, followed by: "What film did you take?"

I said, "Right, what did you do with the package of film after I delivered it?"

"I left it in the car when we changed."

"Where was that?"

"Straight down La Brea, corner of Beverly. He was at the curb in the studio limo. He transferred the man over—that's when he carried him—he put him in my limo, I got in his and drove away. That's the last I saw of it."

"They definitely left the wheelchair in the studio limo."

"I'm pretty sure . . ."

"It *is* a movie," Tony declared. "No *question . . .*"

Roberto lost it then. Not a really together personality there, I think. You see it come out with some people under pressure. He had to lash out at something, knew better than to aim it my way. So he threw an open-hand slap at his pal and shoved him hard against the garage door. Tony came back at him and they had at each other right there, clawing and yelling and rolling all over the place.

Didn't appear as though anyone was going to get hurt seriously in all that, though.

I advised them as they fought, "Don't go to the Springs," and left them to their own disposition.

I didn't know if Roberto could build bombs or not. At the moment it didn't really matter to my agenda. There would be time for Abe Johnson to sort all that later. I left it to his interested ear and went on to Palm Springs. It seemed that it had all begun at the desert. Now I had to try to end it there.

CHAPTER TWENTY-SIX

There were subtleties I didn't have a firm grip on yet, but I thought I had it pretty well figured out by the time I got to the Springs, although I wasn't *sure* of anything. But I was ready to put theory to the heat test, and I had taken it to the only testing ground I had left.

It was shortly after two o'clock on Monday morning when I got there. Temperatures drop quickly on the desert when the sun goes down because the air is usually too dry to hold the heat. Must have been pretty hot that day, though. The temperature was holding at about seventy, downright balmy, with a light wind blowing out of the southeast.

The Mercedes stood in the driveway just outside the garage, same as before, but now the door was down, so I didn't know if the Jag was there. I could not see any lights inside. These condos were built as separate units with maybe six feet of grass between the buildings, two-storied, rear to the street, oddly shaped sides and a sharp pitch to the roofs. So it would be difficult to spot signs of life from the street, anyway. Ditto the other way, unless the garage was open. But something you can usually count on in this area are quiet evenings. I think the average bedtime is about nine o'clock. Sleeping is right up there with golf and tennis as favored pastimes.

I went on by and used the guest parking at the back. The Honda's lug wrench had a wedge at one end, designed for popping off hubcaps—very useful also in various similar applications. I placed it on top of Cassidy's boxfile and took it with me to the Mercedes. Required a couple of quiet pops before I found the vital spot, then it opened the trunk almost as quietly as with a key.

I found bloodied towels and a collapsed wheelchair in there.

Note how the wounded mind operates. I'd been in there with that wheelchair folded up like that. I probably did not actually see it at the time but I experienced it and my mind recorded it as a visual event along with the others; I just didn't select it out.

I opened the wheelchair and put the box in it, pushed it around the side of the building. Lights were on at the front—softly, though, and not providing much illumination. The golf course was right there, the third tee not twenty feet from the condo.

A sliding glass door was open, music was coming from inside, and Charles Franklin sat on a folding chair in the grass. He saw the wheelchair first, then looked up until his eyes were in alignment with mine.

He said, "My God!"

"You keep getting farther away," I told him. "It's still Joe Copp, still doing it the only way I know how."

I had to give the guy credit, he handled it very well—on the surface, anyway. Eyes were a bit wild but voice steady as he said, "Guess there's no such thing as a sure thing."

"That's the only sure thing."

He looked at my gun, quickly looked away from it, took a deep breath. "I guess, as they say, the jig is up."

I kept on my toes, remembering the last time. "I think that's probably true, Charlie. Someone said a little while ago that it would make a great movie. I think you screwed it up, though. Probably a great script but you lost it somewhere."

He looked at the wheelchair with a sour smile. "There's always that one little screwup, isn't there."

"In the movies, yeah. They don't have much time. In real life it's usually a lot of little ones. You've had your share."

"And one of them is standing here with a gun turned on me."

"That's a big one, no question."

"Next time I do my own casting."

"No more next times, Charlie."

"You were the difference," he said. "Of all the private investigators in town . . ."

"I never could follow a script."

"Won't even die on cue, will you. I still don't believe it. Nothing should have lived through that. What are you, a werewolf or something?"

He was talking his senses back. I encouraged it. "Your red herring was great, though. I especially like the Mexico bit."

"Sheer inspiration. I actually did an outline on a

similar idea years ago. Got busy on something else, never developed it. Maybe it would have won an Oscar. You never know."

"Lots of Oscars are lost on the cutting room floor, I hear."

"Oh, before that too. It all begins with the script, you know."

"The writer deserves all the credit?"

"Didn't say that. But the ultimate credit, or ultimate blame. Don't forget that."

"I'm not forgetting it, Charlie. I'm conferring upon you the ultimate blame for this bloody travesty."

"Okay," he said after a moment, "I accept it." After another moment: "I'm curious—do you have a bullet in your head?"

"Ask your stage manager. Or is it the prop man?"

"Prop man . . ."

I was wondering if Franklin had lost his focus. He smiled, though, and said, "Well, nothing ventured, nothing gained. What do we do now?"

"Let's go inside. Do you have a VCR?"

"I think so. Something special you want to see? Justine could probably dig up something fresh for you."

"Brought my own," I told him. "Is she here?"

"Oh yes. And I can't wait to see her face."

Neither could I. "Melissa here too?"

"To be sure."

"You told me nothing's for sure."

He smiled. "That's right, I did. The Baja thing you had twirling, eh? That's good, that's good. Poor dear, I guess it twirled her a bit, too. But after all, we couldn't just kill her."

"Why not?" Nobody else bought a bye."

"Well, true, but not *Melissa*—not at first—I mean,

you could never box office that sympathetically. First we had to try every reasonable alternative."

I wondered if the guy had gone unhinged and actually thought we were discussing a movie script. He seemed really to be getting into it.

"Like," I suggested, "setting her up in Mexico."

"Yes, and we had to make it believable. For *her,* believable. Had to make sense, otherwise she wouldn't want to stay down there. And if she came back too soon . . ."

"Bottoms up?" I suggested.

"Absolutely. Melissa is a dear girl but she's not capable of abstract concepts. She would never have understood about Bernie. Well, you've seen the way she reacted."

"Right. She didn't want to sit there and get blown up with the guy."

"She didn't know that. She simply reacted bizarrely to a minor anomaly. That's characteristic of Melissa. She gets 'vibes,' you see, or thinks she does."

"This time she got lucky."

"Yes, but it wasn't in the script."

"She knew it wasn't Bernie. Why didn't you just tell her it wasn't Bernie. Then you wouldn't have had to blow her up."

"I told you that we tried every reasonable alternative. It finally came to the climactic scene, and Melissa wasn't ready. She would have ruined everything."

"That's what she did."

"I know . . . I knew it would happen this way if we didn't just kill her at the top of the script. I told Justine that. But that woman can be very determined."

The guy had lost it, now I was sure of it.

I picked up the box and pushed him inside the house.

I wanted to see what we had on Butch Cassidy's videocassette.

The pictures I'd taken during my day-long stakeout at *NuCal* were spread across the coffee table like cards in a game of solitaire. Someone had drawn a line from corner to corner with a grease pencil across most of them. A 9mm pistol lay to one side. I scooped up the pistol and dropped it into my pocket.

Franklin sat on the floor beside the TV, back against the wall, looking, I thought, a bit dazed. I loaded in the videocassette and took the remote control to the other wall, the outside wall, and started the play.

Soon as the titles began rolling, Franklin perked up. "Oh, bet I know what this is."

Not many people would. It was a ten-year-old low-budget film produced by Bernard Wiseman. His was the only name I recognized in the credits.

"Shouldn't we call the girls down?" Franklin said.

"In a minute," I told him. "Let's first see what we've got here."

It was an entirely ho-hum production, a bit arty in places but too consciously so. I couldn't decide if it was a romance or a crime melodrama, but I saw a familiar face about ten minutes into it.

"There he is," Franklin said, his voice hushed.

There he sure was.

Could've been a Hitchcock touch.

I froze the picture. "Didn't know Bernie ever appeared in his movies."

"No, he didn't," Franklin said.

"Then who is this?"

"This is . . . Oh! You don't know? Thought you were onto it."

"The stand-in."

"Right. This is Victor Nesmith. Very good character actor. Until a few years ago, of course."

I said, "And a good double."

"Good enough. Right age group, right height and build, little heavier but—we all go up and down. Look at the hairline, though. Perfect, perfect casting!"

"This is the guy that died in the limo."

"With Albert, yes. Poor Albert, he never suspected. Went along with it to the bitter end. Of course it wasn't bitter for him. Never knew what hit him, I'm sure. Don't feel too sorry for him, Albert thought he was in for a share. He wasn't virgin. It was good enough box office, it would play."

"What about Victor Nesmith though?"

Franklin smiled craftily. "Well, you know, he had a pretty good run at it, the role of a lifetime. Don't think he wasn't eating it up. And just when things looked blackest for him. Tell the story from his point of view and you've got a whole new angle on it."

I said, "He was the medical stand-in, too."

"Sure. Here was this very competent actor, down on his luck and I mean way down, not a soul in the world to hold his hand, and he could very easily become a dead ringer for Bernie. Heaven cooperated, that's all."

"Sounds like the Mexican doctors cooperated, too.

Or couldn't they tell the difference between an old and a new injury?"

"Wasn't that old," Charles replied smugly. "Besides, medicine is not that precise a science. Have you ever known three doctors who ever agreed on anything? They see what they expect to see."

I released the freeze and turned off the VCR, told Franklin, "Let's get the girls down here now."

Like Franklin, I was a bit dazed myself. There'd been no accident in Mexico, right, I had that one. But there had been an accident in Burbank two months earlier, and it'd made a paraplegic out of a very competent character actor.

So they had just moved the scene south, rolled the date forward a couple of months, changed the name of the victim, had given him several months secluded in Mexico while he learned his role . . . and behold the new Bernie Wiseman, paraplegic.

Movie magic at its best.

This affair had been brewing for two whole years. And it had been, in its fashion, a brilliant production.

I asked the *auteur,* "Did Victor like Verdi?"

"Loved Verdi," Franklin replied. "We discouraged it, of course. Bernie couldn't tolerate opera."

Of course I'd never met Bernie Wiseman.

CHAPTER TWENTY-SEVEN

They came down the staircase all disgruntled, still half-asleep and wondering what was so urgent to get them out of bed in the middle of the night—attired for the bedroom almost identically in becoming shorty pink babydolls. In most any other circumstances a treat for the male eye, all the golden hair and long bronzed limbs in a ding-dong double for the fantasy-mind. They looked enough alike to be sisters, and in fact, it turned out that they were.

Sleepiness changed to shock when Justine saw the reason for the awakening.

Melissa sank slowly and seated herself on the stairway, trying to focus puffy eyes.

Justine grabbed hold of the rail and leaned back against the wall, settling into a murderous gaze.

Franklin, gloating, informed them: "It's really him. He's not dead. Not even damaged much. How could you miss from that close, Justine?"

Without taking her eyes from me, she said, "What's the matter with you, Charlie? Are you hitting the coke again? What are you talking about?"

"You'd stonewall it to the grave, wouldn't you," I said to her. "Save us all a lot of dumb time. Go put your clothes on, unless you want to get booked in your nightie."

She looked at my gun, looked at Franklin, said to him, "We'll have to write him in."

"How many points?" he said, bargaining about shares like it was still a real unreal scenario.

She looked at me. "You know what's at stake here?"

"Cassidy pretty much told me."

"Learn from his failure, then. Don't get too greedy." She came on down the stairs and settled onto the couch. "Ten points," she said to Franklin, carrying on the movie jargon.

"Probably not enough. Ask him."

I said, "No, it's not enough. But let's talk about it."

I eased Melissa off the staircase and placed her on the couch beside her sister Justine. She pulled away from me. I didn't like the look in her eyes.

"What have you got her on?" I asked big sister.

"Just a little downer, she's under control."

"Can't keep her like this forever."

"We'll have to write her out," Franklin said regretfully. "You know that, Justine."

"Yes, I know it." Regretfully.

"She was blowing a week ago," I pointed out. "Came back and screwed up everything."

Justine gave me a wondering scrutiny. "Have you been in this with Cassidy all the way?"

"We met just recently," I told her.

I took some stuff out of the box and placed it on the

coffee table beside my photos. "Part of his file. You might find it interesting."

She picked up the packet provided by her husband's spy, flipped quickly threw it, tossed it back. "Wasn't interesting the first time I saw it. You keeping those for the wall above your bed?"

"You're very photogenic in any position, but it wouldn't match my decor. I'm not into gruesome."

"Get fucked," she said. Tough.

Franklin said, "Let's settle this about Melissa."

Justine told him, "He hasn't declared himself. Let's get that first."

"Well, maybe he'll be willing to take care of Melissa for you if you make it good enough."

"How do I know what he thinks is good enough? What if he wants it all?"

"He could never have it all, he's smart enough to know that. Make the man a decent offer."

It was very weird. Not only were these people either detached from their senses or totally evil, they were talking about me as though I were somewhere else. Like the director and producer discussing an actor's role in front of him—like he was a pawn. Like I was. I had been for too long . . .

I asked, "Can I get into this story conference?"

"Sure, Joe. We respect your input."

"Thanks. First I need to understand what I *think* I know about the lead characters. Background, motivation, that sort of thing. Melissa, for example, thought she was in Baja being prepped for a major debut. That's okay, I get that angle. But then why was Justine being seen around town as Melissa at the same time?"

"We had to establish Melissa as Bernie's consort,"

Franklin said. "Couldn't just have her appear out of nowhere for the climactic scene."

"Why couldn't Melissa establish that for herself? And then make the switch afterward?"

"Then she would have known he wasn't Bernie."

"No, I mean—" And then it hit me.

Justine said quietly, "Don't tell him anything he doesn't know, for God's sake."

That was okay with me, because now I knew. The "switch" had been made in Mexico two years earlier.

I asked, "How'd you get Albert to wire his own bomb?"

"Don't tell him."

Melissa's eyes were beginning to defog.

Franklin looked at Justine, then told me, "Thought he was wiring it for Roberto. We just changed the timing a bit after he installed it."

I tossed the how-to-bomb book onto the table. "Was Albert a quick study or did he have prior experience with explosives?"

"He learned a lot," Franklin said, "hanging around locations over the years. But these were the first he had built himself. We were proud of him, weren't we," he added to Justine.

I picked up the marked photos. "Who did the trigger work?" I hoped I sounded more casual than I felt.

"Justine," he said, "grew up with guns. Their dad was a trick-shot artist. She can shoot the spades out of an ace at fifty feet. Ironic, isn't it, that she couldn't put a bullet in your brain from half an inch away."

"Closer than that," I said, remembering that moment.

Justine was looking at Franklin with looks that

could kill. About her, that cliché took on fresh impact.

I pinched Melissa's leg and asked Justine, "Do you want to kill your kid sister or don't you?"

I had seen the person coming back in those gorgeous eyes. They looked at me, then shifted with understandable horror to her sister when Justine replied, "How much is it worth to you to kill a whore? I'll give you twelve and a half points and that's final."

"Let's see, that would give me roughly six mil, forty-four between the rest of you. I might go for that but I have to see the money first."

"It isn't just lying about the house, you know," Franklin said. "You'll need to open an offshore account, then we can transfer it in."

"How greedy was Cassidy?"

"Beyond reason. He wanted half."

"You're getting me cheap."

"Well, it's all over now. We're home clean. All *you* have to do is take care of Melissa for us. Do it in Baja. There's a lot of desert down there."

The girl struggled off the couch and lurched toward the door.

Justine grabbed her and tugged her back onto the couch, all but crooned at her, "It's okay, baby, it's okay. We're taking care of you."

I couldn't let it run much longer than that, it was too cruel, too terrifying for Melissa. But I needed a final item.

"Where's Bernie?" I asked Franklin.

"T-three," I thought he said.

"What's that?"

"Tee Three, right outside the door. They were resodding. We planted him there and they sodded him over the next morning."

So Bernie Wiseman had been dead for two years.

I went to the window and gave the high sign. The Palm Springs cops swarmed in and took over. I went out and stood on top of Bernie Wiseman's grave and talked with Abe Johnson, who had brought the cops. They had covered it all from out there with super-pickup directional mikes and hi-tech recorders.

I asked Abe, "Did it pick up okay?"

"Just fine," he assured me. "I have the feeling we're dealing with deranged people here, Joe. At least I'd prefer to think so. I never heard such cold-blooded stuff in all my years as a cop. I'd hate to try taking this case to the prosecutor without this evidence. We'd never make it, they'd laugh us out of court."

"Sorry, Abe, they're not deranged. I don't buy that. Lets them off too easy. They knew exactly what they were doing, *and* they loved it. Like a big game to them. Or a movie production. Take good care of Melissa Franklin, I believe she'll testify for you. And . . . I'd like to be here when you dig up this body."

"Okay, but why?"

"I want to see how lucky I am that this tee was not being resodded Friday night."

He shook his head and went on to join the other officers.

He was right . . . This was a case to shake your head over. A lot of people had died, and death is always unlovely. But the unloveliest part of all was with the principals who were still alive.

If you can call that being alive.

A geek who eats live chickens in a sideshow is alive, I guess. I had to wonder how alive Justine would feel behind bars for even a week without 3-D sexual fantasy to feed her overwhelming appetite.

I was standing by and just sort of hanging loose when they brought Charlie Franklin out with his hands cuffed behind his back and a nearly benign smile on his lips.

"You didn't need it, Charlie," I told him quietly. So why'd you do it?"

"Why not?" he replied casually. "It was fun."

Fun. It was fun.

Be very careful, pal, how you begin to define fun? You could get like Charlie Franklin, or even Justine Wiseman.

Or you could eat live chickens in a sideshow for twelve-and-a-half percent of the gate.

CHAPTER TWENTY-EIGHT

Bernie did have Justine screwed down tight on their premarital agreement—to the effect that she would have been on the street with the clothes on her back and not much more. Of course the California courts have been more than liberal in interpreting such agreements. Bernie was a cagey enough guy to know that she would come out of a court battle with a fair chunk of his net worth unless he had a lot of moral outrage on his side. So he had it all documented before he moved out. He had also cleverly concealed the bulk of his assets, so even in the worst case for him the court would be adjudicating only a small fraction of his actual fortune.

Justine was pretty cagey herself, but she didn't know about what he'd done until after she had killed him. She had gone to Palm Springs in a rage to confront him on the morality issue he was holding over her head. She took a gun with her. Whether by design or not, the confrontation resulted in her husband's death.

And then while he was lying bleeding on the floor, she discovered the truth that he had outsmarted her even in death. By the time the estate was settled, she would get even less than through a divorce settlement.

This was where the game was at when she turned to Charlie Franklin for solace and counsel. They had been friends for years, and apparently Franklin's social bonds to the family were more via Justine than Bernie, in spite of his professed love for Bernie. I think that might have been a crock, anyway.

Charlie seems to have seen the matter as a fun-challenge. He brainstormed it like any other production challenge and came up with what must have seemed the perfect solution. They would bring Bernie back to life, gather back all the concealed wealth and redistribute it in a more equitable fashion—do it all nice and legal and go through the motions of a divorce—then arrange a method by which Bernie's "ghost" could just ride off into the sunset and disappear.

It probably was not thought out much beyond that, in the beginning. There was much to do. They buried the body and found the perfect stand-in to replace it. It even worked out beautifully that the stand-in was recently crippled; they could restage that accident and give themselves plenty of time to work out the details of the impersonation. That developed later as a credible way to keep the new Bernie at low profile in the community—he became a recluse, embittered by his misfortune, showing a face just often enough to maintain the deception. They even kept Bernie's new mansion closed off "pending remodeling" to sink lower that low profile.

Melissa was a threat to the deception, she was considered too unstable to go along with it, and also because Bernie actually had launched plans to launder her past and "discover" her. He had big plans for her, and she knew it.

So they bought her a new car and kept her at a distance with various diversions, thinking that they needed only a few months to nail down the fun-plot and get on with their lives.

Didn't work out that way because the new Bernie also had a studio to run. While trying to pick up the pieces there, they discovered some of the little scams that the real Bernie had been into, mostly nickel-and-dime stuff—but they also saw the opportunity to escalate the scams to a grand slam. It has to be an unexpected and ironic note that most of the recognition as a movie whiz was earned by the *new* Bernie, not the old.

The legitimate estate was worth a few million at most. They found a way to increase it tenfold by abandoning all caution and digging a bit deeper into the skim that was going to the people in New York. They would stall the final accounting and stonewall to the last possible moment—then whisk their man off stage at the best strategic moment.

Of course, that scenario also demanded a much revised game. The stakes were much higher, the penalties for failure too forbidding.

So Franklin rewrote the script and they went for broke.

Melissa was by now becoming a considerable pain so they contrived the game in Baja to keep her out of

their hair. We know how she understood the marriage to Franklin, nutty as it may sound. As for
Charlie's logic, he called it a "control flair," designed
to give him legal leverage "in case we'd want to insti-
tutionalize her." It just wouldn't play, to kill Justine's
own sister unless, of course, they had exhausted all
other possible solutions first. Couldn't "box office" it.

With the escalation, Charlie and Justine had to
bring the new Bernie more into the open, which
meant bringing in additional support—better
makeup, stronger coaching for the acting, various
special effects. And that was where the *NuCal* people
came into it, and they came in with "points." They
also came in with death warrants, because the production company had become too large; it would
have to be dissolved in the final scene because too
many people now knew the truth about Bernie Wiseman.

So that was the way it ran, with Charlie Franklin
as director and executive producer. His well-honed
screenwriter's mind worked at every fine detail and
tried to anticipate the smallest threat to credibility.

Bringing me into it was one of his small "flairs." He
picked me because I'd done some recent work for one
of the street people trying to find and reunite with his
family, and it got a write-up in the paper. Maybe he
figured that made me some kind of bleeding-heart to
go to all that effort for a wino for free. At the least it
satisfied his dramatic sense that I could be counted
on to provide information to the police that would
lead straight to Wiseman, or apparently so.

He wanted to make it look like Bernie was caught
in one of his own little intrigues and overtaken by
retribution from the boys in New York. It was sup-

posed to look as though Bernie had hired me to assist in a plot to silence people who could implicate him in criminal activity. That was the only reason for the formal business deal with the *NuCal* partners, and of course Charlie expected me to come forward when the bombing started. The upshot of it all was to be that Bernie would be blamed for the shooting deaths and the mob would be the prime suspects in the bombing, or vice versa. Almost worked, because Charlie really knew how to "flair" it. He didn't need my photos—just wanted to make it look like Bernie did—the real Bernie posing as someone else. A new twist, no question.

Could have worked. Consider the levels of deception here. Someone claiming to be Bernie, but not Bernie, claimed to be a third party who would ultimately be revealed as Bernie. Flair.

Charlie, by the way, still insists that the original script called for no killings whatever, if one forgot the killing that started it off. But then one thing led to another, rewrite after rewrite, and he claims that Justine "kept getting crazier and greedier."

Redefine "cold-blooded." More than half the deaths were for no reason other than to make credible the final, for-the-record death of Bernie Wiseman.

All the others were to keep the truth in the bag.

Justine killed Forta and Rodriguez, we're sure of that because of the ballistics match. She had probably gone up there to kill me. They surprised her in the house and she shot her way out rather than risk any connection to the other killings, which also were done with her gun.

She killed Edda Swenson, the housekeeper at Wiseman's Bel Air estate, to plug any possible leakage there, then of course she had to kill Edda's daughter, Hulda—the Viking Woman—because she figured the mother's death would not box office with Hulda. I doubt that either victim had knowledge of the deception. With or without that knowledge they were both excess baggage now and needed to be jettisoned. Justine and Hulda were lovers, yes, but that kind of love is easier to replace than wealth and freedom, and that was the only kind of box office that interested Justine.

She killed Butch Cassidy, too. Melissa had already "gone home" looking for sanctuary and told Justine about her midnight date with Guilder and me. It was Justine who insisted that Melissa keep that date, and Guilder must have had one of those leaps of mind when he saw Justine roll in there minutes behind her dead-ringer. Maybe he did panic, or maybe he just had good instincts and knew that he was a marked man. That got Justine worried, though. Melissa had told her that Guilder worked for Cassidy, and Justine knew only too well of Cassidy's interest in the case. So she went to his apartment Friday night after she had dumped me in the desert, cut a deal with him and probably took him to bed. I mention the bed because she left a bomb beneath it.

Must have seemed, though, that they were truly home free after that. Too bad, I guess, that the Aguas couldn't let a white-eyes die in their back yard—too bad for the script, that is.

Charlie Franklin, it seems, has not stopped talking. Seems to enjoy telling it. He's told it to everyone who expresses an interest, even the feds—with eyes on offshore banks and uncollected taxes—and he has told it to members of a New York Crime Commission.

I understand he has told it to a couple of producers, too, so you might even see all this—or a version of it—on the silver screen someday. Speaking of which, Melissa has a new agent who sees no problem at all with her past credits, especially in light of the recent notoriety. She is already considering several offers.

I have not seen Edgar since that night at his place. The charges against me were dropped, and I even got a mention in the press by the heads of both rival police departments.

Abe Johnson came out of it okay, too, I'm glad to say. A hastily scheduled review board rubber-stamped his boss's finding that Abe had "made the proper tactical decision to postpone the apprehension of a suspect (me), which tactical decision led to the apprehension of the true culprits."

I guess it's a wrap, as I believe they say in Hollywood.

I also believe I warned you that this would not be a pretty tale. It got a little prettier after the fact, with Copp remembering how nice it can be just to be alive. I drove down to Baja with Melissa to get some things she had left there. The place had been leased by the new "Bernie" and he still had some time left on the lease, so we didn't feel any need to hurry back to L.A.

Ever do any deep-sea fishing off Baja? Best in the world, they tell me—tarpon and swordfish and all the good stuff—and maybe I'll try it someday. I just didn't have time, not on that visit.

Ever watch the sun set with all those reds and purples as it sinks into an endless blue ocean? Ever see it from a bedroom window when there are only two people alive in the whole world and you can hear both hearts beating and know that one of them belongs to an absolute living doll who would never wish a moment's harm to another living thing?

Ever watch a gracefully naked living doll walk along a deserted beach and stand in private thought with the moon glowing behind her, then turn to you with endlessly blue eyes and a trusting smile?

Ah, yes, life can be beautiful.

It is beautiful.

Fade to black. Roll end titles. It's a wrap.